Thanks for reading this story from the South Dakota prairie. Hope you enjoy it and please know that is fiction. The people and events, as well as the descriptions of the landscape, are straight out of my imagination.

I want to thank my Dakota aunties, Lou Richardson and Betty McMurray, who applied expertise (commas come to mind) and thoughtful suggestions, for their support over the multiple drafts.

A big thank you to my mother, Lois Nicholas, my husband, Buzz, and daughters, Leah and Joanna, who encouraged my efforts to be a "real author". The process is so fun and I'm so grateful to have the time and opportunity to practice the craft.

Jen Nicholas Taylor

February 15, 2019

## Chapter 1

When he didn't find Thomas in the little bunkhouse,
Johnny drove the half mile to the barn. Lights were off in the
little house. He was glad there weren't any dogs on the property.

He turned off the engine and quietly closed the truck door.
The moonlight guided him across the barnyard. He stepped over
the threshold into the black cavernous space, smelling old hay
and horse manure.

"Thomas?" Johnny could hear a faint snort and shuffling.

"Thomas, are you here?" He called again softly into the
darkness.

Johnny lit a match and briefly met the glaze of a horse, her
head hanging over the stall gate. She looked down. He did too.

In the remaining moments of light he saw a body on the
ground before the stall.

"Thomas?"

Johnny kneeled down and placed his cheek over Thomas' mouth but could feel no breath.

"Oh God."


The sun was breaking through the passenger side window of the old truck as Johnny, steering with his left hand, lit a smoke with his right. His fingers were unsteady, holding the glowing red lighter as it made its way to the tip of the cigarette dangling from his lips. While fumbling to return the lighter to its housing in the dashboard, he inhaled deeply. He held the cigarette in two fingers and rubbed his eyes with his thumb and ring finger -- keeping the cigarette butt pointed away from his forehead. He tried to rub out his last vision of Thomas, dead on the cold barn floor.

He needed to see Everett -- and Elsa. They were the last of anything he could call family. He'd moved away after they had married, in the fall after their high school graduation. There hadn't been anything or anyone to hold him in Ree Heights. He'd visited them once or twice over the years, called on the phone occasionally.

Johnny blinked hard and wiped his nose on the sleeve of his shirt.

## Chapter 2

Vera heard the dogs barking and cracked her eyes. It was early -- still shadowy in the corners of her upstairs bedroom. She rolled over and covered her head with a pillow. She wanted to sleep. Sleeping kept thinking at bay. Defeated; the scene of the car accident that killed her parents replayed yet again. Her dad, always a sober driver, had been driving. It was a route he knew well. Vera imagined her parents in the cab of their truck. They would have had the windows cracked if the late April evening had been mild, talking over the day. Vera imagined an infinite variety of details about their final ride. When the train hit, their rig was pushed far down the tracks.

The barking took on a different tone. Vera drug herself out

of bed and moved back a curtain at the window but didn't recognize the blue Ford pickup down in the yard. She pulled on some clothes and hurried downstairs and out the door.

She stepped out onto the back porch to see an older man leaning up against the beat-up truck helping himself to gas from the tank out near the barn. He had his back to her and was bent over the nozzle, focused on the task at hand, seemingly unconcerned about being caught in his thievery.

One of the dogs charged him and she heard a yelp. She crossed the yard in a heartbeat.

"Hey, what the hell are you doin?!" She grabbed his arm and swung him around. Then froze. The man standing in front of her was someone she hadn't seen in nearly twenty years.

"Johnny?" She wasn't entirely sure it was the same man from her early memories. "What are ya doin here?"

Slowly he rested his gaze on her, his eyes puffed and red, the skin on his face sagging around his cheeks and jawline.

Johnny Larson squinted hard and a recognition of the eleven year old girl grown into adulthood dawned in his eyes. "Yeah, well Vera, it's a long story."

He looked away from her and scanned the yards beyond the house. "Where's your dad? I need to talk to him."

The dogs were running around her now. She felt off balance with their barking and movement and with this almost stranger scoping out her property. "It's 5:00 in the morning and you're stealing my gas. What are you doing here, Johnny? What do ya want?"

His face was covered in scruffy gray whiskers and his clothes were dirty. A strong smell of liquor and body odor wafted off of him. His hand shook as he fumbled in a shirt breast pocket for a cigarette. He pulled out the pack but then returned it. His eyes blinked behind his glasses. Again he looked around the yards.

Vera leaned over to rub the heads of the two dogs at her feet. They had stopped barking but were looking up at her face, watching for cues.

Johnny's vision again settled back on her. His voice relayed an urgency. "I need to talk to Everett."

She glanced up at him, then stood up and looked at him directly. "Mom and Dad died in a car accident at the end of April. I'm living on the ranch for the time being."

Johnny slumped against the truck. "God. They're gone? Both of them?"

The dogs were quiet now, settled at her feet, resting but not relaxed.

Vera quickly filled in more of her family's story. "Wally's got his shop in Miller. Coming back from the war and now with the folks dead, he needs some looking after. At least for awhile."

He looked beyond her, across the hills to the south.

In the stillness there were sounds of pigeons stirring in the barn, shaking out their feathers and cooing a good morning to one another.

Johnny turned back to her and took a long look. "Vera,"

his voice shaky, "I'm truly sorry to hear about your folks."

"What are ya doing in Ree Heights, Johnny?" Vera saw him in profile as he turned back around to finish filling his tank. His tightly curled gray hair was matted and covered with a greasy hat pulled low on his forehead. His nose hooked slightly and ended in a moustache, which he chewed on as he concentrated on the task at hand. She asked him. "Are you in some kind of trouble?"

He stepped around her, put the nozzle up, and glanced at her, "Look, Vera, the less you know the better."

He got in his truck and drove out of the yard.

A fine dust kicked up by his truck tires settled back into the driveway.

"What the hell?" She asked the dogs. They looked up at her, tails wagging and tongues hanging out.

As she headed for the house, a sense of aloneness swept over her. In the space of a few weeks, she had traded her vibrant life in the city for a solitary existence. Over the years, she had, more than once, tried to explain to her city friends the sense of vastness out on the prairie. How the wind blows, day in and day out, and often throughout the night. How the landscape is mostly flat, like a table-top, with virtually no trees and how the weather can be extreme, temperatures dropping sometimes to minus 20 degrees and below in the winter and breaking upwards of 110 degrees in summer. She often felt that she wasn't doing the Great Plains justice and that she wasn't being believed.

She heard cattle mooing in a nearby pasture and could smell barnyard odors mixed with plum trees blooming in the tree strips. Along with the hollowed out feeling of emptiness, she was surprised to find the twin feelings of independence and self-reliance bubbling up to make this familiar life that she has returned to something more than what she remembered.

The dogs followed her back in the house and flopped down in the middle of the small kitchen. Vera stepped over and around them to pick up the phone. She listened for a moment on the party line then dialed her Aunt Leona.

"Leona, you'll never guess who came by this morning and helped himself to gas."

Leona snorted. "You calling at 6:00 in the morning to report stolen gas?"

"You remember Johnny Larson?"

Vera heard a sharp intake of breath.

"Sounds like some static on the line, Vera," Leona quipped. "Better come on into town."


Leona was watering her garden when Vera drove up and parked in front of her aunt's aging, two-story home located on the edge of Ree Heights. Leona's husband had died years ago. He and Leona had raised three kids in the old house and ranched sections of land bordering the small town. Between careful management of inherited acres and a frugal lifestyle, they had managed to become somewhat prosperous in the ranching business where few could make that claim.

Vera breathed in the fragrant scent of apple blossoms as

she walked over to the long garden. Leona planted at the end of March no matter what, though there were years when a late spring blizzard covered her garden. Now in early June, she was harvesting lettuce, spinach, and radishes.

Vera gave her aunt a smile. "Your garden's looking good, Leona."

Leona was leaning on a hoe. "Let's go in, Vera. I could use a rest."

Vera watched as Leona, with a steadying hand on the crumbling stucco siding, leaned down and turned off the hose then followed her up the back steps and into the high-ceilinged kitchen.

While Leona washed up, Vera found cups in the china cabinet and poured them both coffee. She helped herself to a cinnamon roll, warm from the oven and cooling on a wire rack. She leaned against the long kitchen counter devouring the roll.

Leona dropped down in a kitchen chair, pulling out another to put her feet up.

"Is your arthritis bothering you, Leona?"

"Getting old ain't for sissies." Leona flexed her fingers then frowned at Vera. "What's all this about Johnny Larson."

Vera set her cup on the table and sat down across from her aunt. "Johnny was down in the yard helping himself to gas. At the crack of dawn I might add."

Leona finished wiping her glasses and secured them on her face. "What the hell is that old coot doing back in this area?"

"He wasn't looking too good." Vera blew across the top of the steamy coffee. "Old and worn out. Ragged looking. Stinky."

With a puzzled look Leona said. "I think he was out to visit your folks not that long ago? Maybe in February?"

"Yeah, I don't know." Vera shrugged. "I don't recall them mentioning a visit from Johnny."

She got up, picked up the coffee pot and refilled both of their cups. "I had intended to get home more often, ya know, but things really heated up at work in the past year."

Vera had left her hometown after high school seeking a

freedom from the microscope of her childhood. The good parts of the blanket of attention and affection piled on by relatives and well-intentioned neighbors as she grew up could, at times, feel oppressive. When she would come back to Ree Heights for a visit, she'd enjoy herself but was always ready to get back to the anonymity of the city.

Sitting in Leona's old kitchen, memories of a wild childhood with her cousins -- one with little supervision -- came to mind. She knows now they could only have had that sort of untamed independence because of the safety net provided by those small-town caregivers who saw to their well-being, whether they liked it or not.

"You can guess that snake is up to no good." Leona muttered.

Vera's thoughts were pulled back to the present with Leona's comments.

"He's got some history here, huh?" Vera baited her aunt.

Leona's face took on a sour look. "Johnny used to pull your

dad into trouble when they were teenagers."

"From the stories I've heard about Dad, I don't think he needed much prodding from Johnny?" Vera mused.

Leona pursed her lips and glared. "I don't like it. Him coming around here now."

"Do you know what he wanted from Dad when he was here in February?" Vera had her own memories of Johnny disrupting the tranquility of their family.

"I believe Elsa said he was in the area checking on business contacts he had down at Crow Creek." Leona responded then took a moment to study Vera's face.

"Really?" Vera's eyebrows furrowed. "Did Mom say anything about who that might have been or what he was up to?"

Vera waited for her aunt's reply.

"Don't recall." Leona seemed to be pushing away memories as she stood up, holding the side of the table to get her balance. She wobbled over to the sink to set her cup down.

Talking over her shoulder, Leona continued. "I'm going to

go get changed for church. We're sharing a minister this summer with a Highmore parish. His sermons are short."

Vera got up from the table and stood alongside Leona, rinsing out her cup at the sink. She gently nudged Leona's shoulder. "Are you drumming up business?"

"It wouldn't kill you, girl." Leona raised an eyebrow.

"Ha. Ya sure about that?" Vera grinned. "Thanks for the coffee and roll. Guess I'll head over to Miller to check on Wally."

Leona moved down the counter and covered a plate of rolls with plastic wrap and handed it to Vera. "How bout you take these to him?"

Vera smiled again. "Thanks Leona."


"Wally?" Vera called into the open garage door.

Their parents had sold a section of land to buy the shop for Wally while he was in Vietnam. Maybe it was their way to ensure his safe return. In the months after he had come back from the war, the shop had been a haven for him -- a refuge he seldom left. He seemed to need the solitude and routine of the shop to tame the demons rattling through his mind.

She saw a pair of boots sticking out from under a vehicle up on jacks. Leaning over the raised hood, she addressed the top of the engine. "Leona sent over some rolls for you."

Wally rolled out from under the car and looked up at Vera. His face relaxed into a slow smile.

They moved out to the front of the building, settling on inverted crates to lean back against the warming brick wall. Wally balanced the plate of pastry on his lap as he ate. The few houses near the shop were quiet in the early morning. Vera felt her shoulders relax and her eyelids droop.

She rolled her head to study her brother's profile. Handsome with blond hair and fair features, he was big-boned with a squared off chin like their Dad's. "Hey, Wally, you get a haircut? Looks good."

Wally glanced at her then looked away. "Yeah."

It was quiet again but for the meadowlarks calling from the nearby field, building their nests.

Vera cracked open her eyes and again looked at her brother. "You remember Johnny Larson? He came to visit us a couple of times."

He shrugged. "I don't think so."

"You probably too young to remember, but one time he flew in and parked his airplane in the yard." She added.

Wally ate the last roll.

"He was on the ranch early this morning helping himself to gas."

"What did he want?" Wally lowered his crate down to the ground.

"He didn't say much." Vera accepted the empty plate from Wally. "He didn't know that Mom and Dad had died."

Wally looked at her briefly and nodded, then stood up and moved back to the raised Camaro.

Vera stood up and followed him into the shop.

Wally seated himself on the low gurney. He lay down and rolled back under the car.

Vera leaned over and spoke to the underside of the Camaro. "Wally, come out to the ranch later and I'll make us supper?"

"Uh maybe." His reply muffled up through the engine block.

She gently kicked one of his boots. "I'll see ya later."

Vera hoped that her stay in Ree Heights could be short term, hoped her brother's mental health was stabilizing. A matter of a few months? She couldn't wait too long to return to her life in Minneapolis.

## Chapter 3

Vera was back in the house and starting coffee when the phone rang.

"Morning Vera." It was a raspy smoker's voice and it took

her a moment to place Thelma, the Hand County Sheriff's dispatch.

Her employment with the Hand County Sheriff department had begun only a few days ago. With bills piling up, she needed a source of income. Earl Adams, the Hand County sheriff and an old friend, had hired her, said they needed a second deputy. With a 1,400-square-mile area to cover, the calls coming in on the west and south parts of the county were now Vera's responsibility.

"Hey Thelma. What's going on?" Vera had a hard time hearing her over a dog yapping in the background. Vera remembered that Thelma picked up calls coming into the sheriff's office on evenings and weekends from her house. Working for the county sheriff was a far cry from her job with the Minneapolis Police Department, but she was grateful for the work.

"I just took a call from Franklin Hasart. He sounded real upset."

"What's going on?" Vera heard some breathing on the line.

Another difference between her job in the city and her new position with the county sheriff.

"I'm not sure, Vera. Can you go down there?" Thelma must have heard the breathing too. "Call me back when you can."

Vera changed into her sheriff-issued buttoned-down shirt, poured coffee into her thermos then started down the blacktop road that runs south out of Ree Heights through the Ree Hills. Both the town and hills were named for the Ree Indians, a woodlands tribe. The Arikara, as they were also called, had been some of the earliest inhabitants of the area.

Vera glanced at the dogs in the back seat of her VW Bug. Each had a head hanging out a window, tongues flapping in the wind. She relaxed into the gently rolling countryside and breathed in the first cutting of hay. A tractor was parked in the middle of a hay meadow on this day of rest while beehive-shaped hay stacks left from past years, gray and crumbling along the fence line.

Eventually, she turned off the blacktop onto a dirt drive,

the washboard surface slowing her progress. Bumping along, she recalled spending an afternoon on the ranch years ago with her friend, a granddaughter of Franklin and his wife, Wilma. Their property shared a border with the Crow Creek reservation. When she drove into the yard, she saw a bent figure standing in front of a tribal police officer, gesturing with his cane in the direction of the barn.

Vera parked under a big cottonwood, told the dogs to stay in the car, and joined the two men.

Franklin recognized her. "Vera, glad you're here. I was just telling him," pointing with his chin to the tribal officer, "about Thomas."

She looked to the officer and her throat tightened.

It had been twelve years since she had last seen James Broken Hand. They had dated the summer after their high school graduation. From different ends of the county, their high schools had been rivals in sports as their ancestors had been rivals for the land. It had been a romance disapproved by many in her community. Their relationship had ended abruptly when she left him without saying goodbye.

James nodded in her direction. "Hello Vera."

"James." She waited for her heart to resume a regular beat, then asked, "What's going on?"

"A man who works for Franklin is dead." James answered.

"Let's go, Franklin." James turned toward Franklin who headed toward the barn. Vera followed.

Franklin led the way slowly through the dimly lit, cool interior to where a body lay curled up in fetal position on the barn floor.

James knelt down for a closer examination. "This is Thomas Yellow Knife. I know his family."

He looked up at the old man leaning heavily on his cane. "When did you find him, Franklin?"

Franklin's voice cracked. "I come out to milk this morning and found Thomas just there."

Kneeling on the other side of the body, Vera could see no

visible signs of violence. Nothing obvious that could explain his death. In faded blue jeans and a plaid shirt tucked neatly into his jeans, Thomas looked to be his mid-to-late teens.

She looked over her shoulder to ask. "When was the last time you saw him alive, Franklin?"

"Evening yesterday." Franklin blew his nose and added, "He helped me with chores."

"How long has Thomas been working for you?" James stood to listen to Franklin's response.

"He started this spring. Helped me with the calving. He stayed on to help with haying."

Vera stayed kneeling next to the body as she listened to Franklin. There was a sort of tenderness about Thomas that made her catch her breath. His face was light brown and smooth. His long slightly wavy hair was a deep red-brown color and pulled back into a ponytail.

Franklin offered more details. "Thomas has been living

down in the little house since he graduated from high school."

Vera knew that the Hasarts, like many ranchers in the area, provided seasonal housing for their hired men.

"Was Thomas the only person living there right now?" Vera stood up to face Franklin.

Franklin kept his eyes on Thomas' body. "Nobody else was living there. Just Thomas."

Kneeling down again, James laid a beaded leather thong near the body and quietly spoke a few words in Lakota.

He stood up and returned his cowboy hat to his head.

He glanced at Franklin then looked back at the body. "Do you know if Thomas left the ranch last night? Or if he had company out here with him?"

Franklin shrugged his shoulders, making his stoop more pronounced. "Me and Wilma go to bed early, ya know. I don't know if he was off the place last night."

Franklin shook his head slowly. "I just don't understand how Thomas could be dead."

"We need to call the coroner, Franklin." Vera used the gentle voice she had cultivated over years working with domestic abuse cases in the city. "Can I use your phone?" The request moved him out of his stupor.

Vera and James followed him out of the barn.

In the house, Vera placed a call to the county coroner, Albert Phinney.

She hung up, then looked up, meeting James' questioning gaze. "He's on his way. But it'll take him awhile to get out here."

"Let's go take another look around?" James suggested.

She noticed her stomach hurt a little. She took a deep breath and reminded herself to get a grip. She needed to keep her head in the game.

## *Chapter 4*

Out of the daylight, the darkness in the barn took a few minutes to adjust to. James and Vera moved without speaking to where Thomas' body lay.

James looked across the body at her. "I heard you were living back in the area."

Hearing his voice, memories of their summer together flooded back. Just out of high school, Vera had been restless and eager for change. James had helped to satisfy some of those feelings that summer they spent together. But she also remembered the harsh and even hostile reactions to their relationship she had encountered in her community, comments that confused and embarrassed her, by the people she thought she knew and trusted.

She had broken it off with James, had vowed to leave the area and never return. After attending college in eastern South Dakota, she'd moved to a life outside the state. She had always regretted not telling him why she left.

Standing in the dark barn over a dead teenager all the feelings from over a decade ago flooded over her. She realized the years away from Ree Heights had neither diminished the disappointment she felt about some in her community nor the

25

feelings she had for James.

She stared into the space above his shoulder, watching how the sunlight, shaped by the barn door, outlined dust and bits of hay floating in the air.

"Real sorry to hear about your parents, Vera." James spoke quietly.

She squinted up at him, the mix of past memories and the present reality making her slightly dizzy. "Yeah, it was a shock. The car accident."

She blinked hard and looked back down at the young man laying on the barn floor, then added, "I'm only back temporarily, until I can get things sorted."

They turned their attention to the crime scene. James squatted down and gently rolled Thomas' body over. He started going through his pockets, handing her Thomas' wallet.

She studied his driver's license and commented, "Thomas just had his eighteenth birthday. Older than he looks."

In a back pocket James found a brochure for a community

college located in Denver and in a front pocket a house key, a candy wrapper and a coin. These items he placed in a plastic bag. Vera added the wallet to the bag.

"Any ideas about how he died?" Vera sat back on her heels. "Looks like he just curled up for a nap. Strange."

"There is something around his mouth." James looked closely but avoided touching the skin. She noticed the flecks of dark brown.

Vera glanced at James. "Do you know the family well?"

With her own recent experience of death, Vera could easily imagine the pain and loss for Thomas' family when hearing about his death. The death of her parents had been a shock to the entire town. The way she saw it, each person holds a space in a small community and when that person is removed -- either through death or departure -- there is a hole, a void. The group must rearrange and rebuild itself. Like Ree Heights, Fort Thompson was a small community where a death would leave a vacuum. An unexplained death might cause an uneasiness that could lead to suspicion and fear.

"I know Thomas' Aunt Betty." James rubbed his chin, sighed, and looked at Vera. "His death will be hard on her. She's in her late eighties. Thomas has lived with her since he was very young."

They carefully examined the immediate area and nearby stalls. Vera rubbed the nose and patted the neck of a very pregnant mare. "Too bad she can't tell what she's seen."

They walked out into the main part of the old barn. Vera led the way up uneven wooden steps into the haymow. Pigeons burst out from perches in the rafters and exited the wide door at the end of the mow.

"Smells just like I remember," Vera commented.

"Guess you haven't been in a barn in about twelve years?" James replied.

She looked quickly at him, wondered if he was the remembering the last time they were in a haymow together.

They walked the length of the mow to the ledge of the

opening. It was a view of an unoccupied barnyard, board fences sagging and manure piles in the corners. Two milk cows grazed in a nearby pasture while red and white Hereford cattle and their calves dotted the pastures in the distance.

James glanced at her before moving off. "Pretty peaceful if ya like a rural lifestyle."

Vera turned from the scene a minute later and followed him down the steps, out of the barn, and up to the old house.

"Come in." Franklin waved them in through the screen door. He was seated at the kitchen table, his wife, Wilma, had her hand on his shoulder.

Wilma brought them mugs of coffee, then joined them at the kitchen table. It was quiet for a space of time then Franklin began a retelling of the events.

"I went out to milk this morning. Thomas was lying there so quiet." Franklin talked into a middle space. "I thought he was sleeping. I went to him and tried to wake him."

"No doubt it was a shock to find Thomas dead." James

responded.

Franklin looked at James with something like relief and gratitude.

James added, "Seems like you and Wilma enjoyed having Thomas working here for you?"

"Thomas was a kind young man," Wilma dabbed her nose with a handkerchief. "He didn't go to town except to see his auntie. He didn't go out like some young folks to drink and what not."

She continued, "One day a couple weeks after he started working for Franklin, Thomas come up to the house carrying a little kitten. Said it looked like the mama cat had moved on." Wilma moved her coffee cup between her two hands, keeping her focus on the cup. "Thomas wondered did I want to keep the little thing up here at the house? Oh no, I said, maybe you should keep that kitten."

Wilma looked up at her audience. "Ya know, he just grinned and said he'd like that. Taking care of that little kitten."

She pulled her handkerchief out of the sleeve of her sweater and wiped her eyes.

Vera reached over and patted the old woman's hand.

Through the kitchen window they saw Albert pull up in his old station wagon.

James stood up, holding his hat between his two hands. "You take care now, Franklin, we'll find out what happened to Thomas."

He nodded toward Wilma. "Thanks for the coffee."

Vera stood too. "I'll call you when we find out more." She let the screen door close gently as she looked back at the kitchen table.

Albert stepped out of the vehicle with his small brown leather bag and nodded to Vera and James. "Please show me the body."

Albert was the only man in the county Vera knew who wore a suit jacket and a fedora. The jacket was ancient and the fedora well broken in, but Vera thought the ensemble gave him a certain gravitas in situations that benefited from the weight of his expertise.

Albert walked slowly around the body then looked at the two officers. "Did you move him at all?"

"Just to roll him over," James explained.

"And look through his pockets," Vera added.

Albert pulled on gloves and asked, "When was the body found?"

"About 6:00 this morning," James responded.

Vera finished the answer. "By Franklin."

He scrutinized Thomas' fingernails and lips, then pulled up an eyelid for examination.

"OK," he said. "Please go and get the stretcher to remove the body."

Vera wasn't sure, but thought he might be talking to her. She looked over at James who gave her a half-smile and a bit of a "who knows" head tilt.

She brought the stretcher from the back of Albert's station wagon and laid it out beside the body, then together Vera and James lifted the body onto the stretcher and carried it to the back of the vehicle.

Albert, meanwhile, walked briskly from the barn, opened the car door, and slid into the driver's seat.

He turned his head slightly in the direction of Vera and James who were standing nearby and said through the open window, "I will call when I have discovered something."

He drove slowly out of the yard.

James walked with Vera over to her car. She stole another quick look at him. Just under six feet with a lean muscular build, his hair was cut short under his hat. Still handsome, she thought, the crow's feet around his eyes added to his attractiveness. She noticed he walked with a limp and wondered what had happened.

Vera let the pups out to run to a nearby tree. They were back in a flash to greet James. He obliged with petting. They reciprocated with excited tail wagging and full body wiggling.

James had the evidence bag in his hand. Removing the wallet, he said, "I'll go by and see Thomas' auntie. Give her his wallet."

She took the bag from him. "I can call the community college in Denver."

James leaned against the roof of the VW and wrote down his phone number on a piece of paper. Handing it to her, he said, "Give me a call when you find out something."

Her fingers brushed his as she accepted it. "I will."

She glanced up at him quickly, then opened a back door for the dogs and they hopped in. She climbed into the driver's seat and pulled her door closed.

James leaned down, resting his forearms along the open window. "So you're staying on the home place, then?" he asked her.

His face was in shadow from the tree branches overhead but his voice was the same quiet and sure voice she remembered from years ago. She stared at his hand resting on the window frame then looked up at him and nodded.

James stood up, holding her gaze for a moment before turning away. "I'll see ya later."

Vera felt a flutter of anticipation as she watched him walk off to his pickup. She sighed deeply then gave her head a shake. Her life was complicated enough as it was. And things may have just gotten more complicated. She was almost certain she recognized the coin they found on Thomas' body.

## Chapter 5

The dogs were thirsty when Vera drove up into the house yard. They headed to the horse trough for a drink and a dip. With the mid-day temperatures starting to rise, Vera closed down the windows in the little house to keep the hot wind from blowing through it. She was looking in her fridge for a lunch when the phone rang.

"Is this Vera? Wally's sister? I think you need to get over here. Your brother's pretty upset."

Leaving the dogs, she jumped back in her car. She couldn't remember what name the person had given her, only that she was Wally's neighbor. Oh god. What was going on? How was she going to move back to her life in Minneapolis if her brother couldn't get well? If he couldn't function without her? She really couldn't stay in Ree Heights.

She drove the old gravel road to Wally's shop at the edge of Miller, slowed and parked. She saw Wally's neighbors from across the street standing out on their porch. She gave them a quick wave.

Wally was cursing and pacing in the open bay of his shop.

"Wally. Hey Wally." She called to him softly.

She approached him and touched his arm.

He looked up from his rant, disoriented. "Vera. He stole my rifle."

"Who stole your rifle?" She asked.

He focused on her face, his eyes furrowed, confused.

"Come on, Wally. I'll make us some coffee." She led him

into the back of the shop where he had his living quarters.

Sitting at the small formica table and sipping the coffee, Vera waited until Wally was ready to talk about what happened.

Wally stared down into the cup. "I was working under the Camaro when I heard a car door slam."

Vera asked quietly, "When was that Wally?"

"About an hour or so ago I guess." Wally was slowly losing steam. "I got out from under the car in time to see the son of bitch drive off with my rifle."

"Could you see who it was? Did you recognize him?" Her lips were pressed together as she studied his confused face.

"Goddamn him, Vera. He stole Dad's old 22. It can't be worth much except to me."

He wasn't drinking, but was holding onto the cup.

"You remember the time I took that skunk with it?" He looked up at her.

"Yeah, I remember the skunk that wintered under the shed." Vera's vision was blurring.

He continued, "That was the first time I used it. Dad set me up, talked me through the shot."

They didn't talk about their shared grief, the daily ache of missing their parents. Vera brushed at her wet cheeks then reached over to rest her hand on Wally's arm. His head was down, chin resting on his chest.

"Wally, we'll get it back." She wanted to reassure him.

With a nine year age gap, she looked at him now and saw in him the younger, vulnerable brother who needed her to look out for him.

Vera left him for a minute to step outside. She called to the older neighbors who were now sitting on chairs on the porch. "Wally's going to be fine. Sorry for the commotion."

When she returned to the back of the shop, she found Wally with his elbows on the tabletop and his head between his hands. She tried to give him a bit of a hug but he didn't look up.

She had asked him what the man looked like but hadn't gotten a response -- now she asked. "Wally, did you see the car he was driving?"

He looked up, his expression bleak but certain. "Yeah, Vera, he was driving a blue Ford pickup."

Vera's features hardened.

## Chapter 6

Vera stewed on the ride back to the ranch. She needed to find Johnny. What was he doing in the county and why would he steal Wally's rifle? It didn't make sense. He had seemed so defeated this morning.

As she parked her car in front of the house and turned off the motor, she heard the sound of a vehicle pulling up behind her.

She got out and walked back to talk with the occupant of the brand new white Chevy pickup.

"Hello, Mr. Martin." She talked to him through his open window.

"Hello little lady." Francis Martin, a years-ago transplant

to Hand County from somewhere in Texas, spoke with a left-over southern drawl.

He looked quickly at her before resuming his survey of the property. "Looks like the upkeep of the ranch is proving to be a hardship for you, Vera."

"Oh I wouldn't say that." She looked around.

Thankfully, the early summer greenery masked the minimal amount of work she had done in the upkeep of the place. By the end of August, though, the hot dry winds of summer would expose the work she had neglected.

"Donnie White is working with me. We're doing all right."

"Donnie's got health problems, I guess you know that? And with his own place to work, he won't be able to do much more for you in the future."

"I'm learning as I go, Mr. Martin." Vera's arms were folded across her chest; she looked at the ground and kicked at a rock.

"Missy." His voice was sharper. "You need to consider the very reasonable offer I've made to buy this ranch."

Francis Martin had moved to the area two decades ago and amassed a fortune from others' misfortune. Vera did not intend to be included in his windfall.

She raised her head and met his eye. "Again, thank you for the offer but I am not selling the ranch."

He scowled at her. "Young lady, this offer will be withdrawn as some point and you will be sorry."

With the cost of gas going up, the ongoing drought, and the rising interest rates, her parents had gotten behind in paying back the bank loans. Mr. Martin's purchase of the ranch would be a step closer toward her freedom and away from the situation she had found herself in, but she knew he was low-balling her.

"I'll keep your offer and its deadline in mind."

The truck threw up gravel as Francis Martin left in a hurry. Vera released a sigh. She never imagined herself running the ranch. If she really stayed, it would be a steep learning curve to becoming a successful rancher. As it was, she was counting on Donny and Leona to guide her through the decisions that needed to be made now and hoped to make the money to pay back the bank loan in November. Then she would think about putting the ranch on the market.

## Chapter 7

The sun was warming up the grassy hillsides and reaching into the dark tree-lined draws as James drove back to Fort Thompson from Hasarts' ranch. He saw a coyote crest a hilltop, stop, look, then trot along a trail.

He took a deep breath and unclenched his jaw. He dreaded having to inform Thomas' family of his death. James wanted Howard, the younger brother of Betty Yellow Knife, along when he broke the news of Thomas' death to her. In his upper 70's, Howard held his family -- and in many ways, the tribe -- together. James respected and valued the role Howard played in their community.

Although born in the early 1900s when the Sioux tribes had already been confined to reservations, Howard had grown up hearing the stories of their life on the plains. A life of shared community and customs; a life of freedom and honor; a life before white settlers and soldiers. His memories of their ancestors and those stories served to connect the people with their traditions, language and culture. He remained a living link from the past to the present.

James slowed to cross a cattle-guard. Further down the fenceline he saw a mother cow had stretched her neck to rub the underneath of it on a fence post; nearby her calf lowered his head and kicked his heels.

Their past was a bruised history. The treaty of 1868, meant to recognize the Black Hills as a part of the Great Sioux Reservation and signed between the US government and the Sioux tribes living on the South Dakota plains, was quickly broken in 1874 when General George Custer led gold prospectors into the Hills. Skirmishes between federal troops and Native tribes continued until the federal government took possession of the Black Hills in 1877. The scattered tribes were hunted down and rounded up onto reservations.

Nine reservations checkerboard the South Dakota landscape. Five of the reservations are located along the Missouri River which bisects the state. At the north end of the state and extending into North Dakota is the Standing Rock Reservation. Standing Rock shares a border with the Cheyenne River Reservation to its south. Continuing along the Missouri, the Lower Brule Reservation is located on the west side of the river and Crow Creek Reservation on the east side. Further south along the river is the Yankton Reservation, which borders the Nebraska state line. In the southwestern part of the state, and adjacent to each other, are the Pine Ridge and Rosebud Reservations. The Traverse Lake Reservation, home of the Sisseton Wahpeton Oyate, forms a pie wedge in the northeast corner. A small square, south of Sisseton and nestling the Minnesota border, is the Flandreau Santee Reservation.

Tribal lands were further reduced in the 1940s when additional tracts of land were taken by the federal government in order to build dams and hydroelectric plants along the Missouri River. Nearly 22,000 acres of the Crow Creek and Lower Brule reservation land were flooded as a result. Fertile land for growing alfalfa and pastures used for grazing livestock as well as native trees and medicinal plants were lost in the flooding.

James knew that Howard, along with others in the path of the flooding, had been forced to adapt to the changes. With his ranch underwater, Howard had had to find other ways to support his family. Over the years, as many in the Crow Creek tribe felt the effects of forced breaks in their traditional lifestyle and a loss of tradition and culture, they turned to Howard to provide a connection to their shared past. His steady demeanor projected calm.

James was grateful for Howard's quiet, unshakable personality now. Betty needed him. James knew the community would come together to support her too, bringing food and companionship, in this time of sadness and mourning.

# Chapter 8

Lucas was waiting for him on the front step, wearing cowboy hat and boots, and playing with the cat.

"Dad! Let's go!" Lucas jumped up and ran to his dad.

James scooped him up in a hug. "Glad to see you're ready, Lucas. I'm going to go talk with Aunt Sandra for a minute. You can get in the truck."

James made his way through the small house to the kitchen where he found his sister working at the counter. Bread, packages of meat and cheese, an open bag of potato chips, and a jar of homemade pickles covered the surface. Head down, she was spreading mayonnaise and mustard on bread slices.

"Thanks for staying with Lucas this morning." He opened a cabinet for a glass, stepped around her to run water in the sink.

He filled his glass then looked again at her. Her motions were stiff. "What's up, Sandra?"

She turned to James with a worried look. "I've been

hearing some rumors."

James drank the water and reached for a chip. "Rumors about what?"

Sandra turned around to face him. "About AIM. About how more and more of them are coming. Coming to stir things up."

James pulled out another chip. "You'd think with a name like American Indian Movement they'd take their anger to Washington, not to the reservations?"

She shot him a frown.

James crossed his arms, studied her face in profile and said. "I've heard some rumblings about AIM coming for the past few months but it doesn't seem to amount to much. Mostly talk."

Sandra slapped together sandwiches as she talked. "You know as well as I do that over on Pine Ridge there are plenty of people who are sick and tired of the tribal government strong-arming people. What with Ray Jackson winning the tribal president seat in a rigged election and then cutting sweet deals with the feds for himself and his relations. Anger's been building."

She began loading the lunches in a paper bag. "Word is AIM is already camped over at Pine Ridge and Rosebud. That they are bringing weapons onto the reservations, that they're ready to start a rebellion."

As he listened to her, James remembered past conversations with his sister where she had pointed out his naivety. Sandra could smell trouble coming.

Blindly trusting Martha, Lucas' mother, had been one charge she had unloaded at him a few years ago. She said Martha was a phony and a manipulator. That was certainly true.

Years ago, she had also warned him off dating Vera. She'd said that Vera was flighty. That she would break his heart. And that happened.

"From what I'm hearing rifles are coming into Crow Creek too." Sandra glanced at her brother, saw she had his full attention. "Soon."

She faced him and continued with a sigh. "You're not going to like this next part. It sounds like Martha has been in contact with her cousin Leonard. Word is she's gotten involved with AIM."

"There's more, James." Her voice quivered. "Leonard is telling people Martha's coming back to get Lucas."

"What?" His eyebrows furrowed and his mouth tightened. "She's not taking him anywhere. That'll be over my dead body."

"She left over a year ago. She's probably just blowing smoke." James didn't seem to hearing her, but Sandra continued. "Weapons into Crow Creek could just be rumors too? But this morning, down at the center, the elders were talking about it."

James refocused on Sandra's face and shook his head slowly. "I just thought it was going to stay at the grumbling level here."

Sandra pitched her voice to sound reassuring. "There're enough level-headed people in this community to keep open warfare from happening."

"God, I hope you're right." James sighed.

He stood at the sink and stared out the window. "Does Martha really think she can breeze back onto the reservation and take Lucas?"

Sandra moved to stand next to him. "Listen, you better get going. Mom and Dad are expecting you and Lucas. Here." She handed him the paper bag.

"Thanks, Sandra." He took a big breath and let it out slowly. "You're working tomorrow?"

"Yep. Until Thursday."

He could see Lucas waiting for him in the passenger seat, window rolled down, and could hear his son talking to the cat who was sitting on the ground below the window, licking herself. "We're going to a rodeo, Lulu. Gonna see Gramma and Grampa."

James came around the truck and got in with the paper bag. "Aunt Sandra made us sandwiches -- your favorite -- bologna with mustard."

James backed the truck up out of the yard while Lucas was up on his knees, his head hanging out the window, saying bye to the cat.

He turned his head around to ask, "Dad, can we get still get fry bread when we get there?"

A mere mention of fry bread caused James to salivate. Any gathering on the reservation -- be it a family get together, a powwow and dancing, or a rodeo -- always included a vat of sizzling hot oil with a mounded heap of dough ready to pinch off and fry up. James remembered his grandmother telling him about how, when the tribe was forced onto reservation lands, they used the government rations of flour, salt, baking powder, and lard to make fry bread. "Ya might say they made some lemonade," she would say about her people. James liked his fry bread topped with his mom's chokecherry jelly -- a recipe handed down in his family.

"Course we can get fry bread." James leaned over and grabbed at an ankle. "Hey, sit down, bud. Don't want ya falling out the window."

They drove slowly through town waving at people out on a Sunday morning. Lucas called to a friend from his kindergarten class playing in a ditch of standing water left from a heavy rain earlier in the week. His friend looked up from the muddy stream where he was floating boats of wood bark and waved.

James drove with his hands tightly clenched on the steering wheel, thinking about his conversation with Sandra.

He slowed down, suspicious, then recognized the two young men sitting on an old car parked at the basketball courts, smoking cigarettes and hanging out.

He squinted to read an out-of-state license plate on a vehicle parked in front of the grocery store. He shook his head, trying to clear his growing paranoia.

The road out of Fort Thompson and the Crow Creek Reservation dropped down from the bluffs that bordered the river and crossed the Missouri River into the Lower Brule Reservation.

Lucas loved this part of the ride where the bridge spanned the wide river and he could see down into the swirling waters and along the banks.

"Dad! I saw a fish jumping!"

"Dad! There's a guy fishing down there!"

Once across the river, Lucas quieted down, leaned his head back against the seat and watched the countryside roll by his window.

James glanced at his son's drooping eyelids and smiled.

Moving across the open landscape, James let his mind drift back to the morning's surprise encounter with Vera. He'd heard that she'd moved back to the ranch after the death of her parents. He hadn't known she was working for the Hand County Sheriff, but it made sense. He knew she worked in law enforcement in Minneapolis.

The images of her from the morning were pleasantly distracting. She'd filled out, in a nice way. She was an average height but, and he remembered this detail from their summer together, depending on the occasion, she could seem taller. Today though, she had seemed smaller, more fragile. She seemed to carry herself with more reserve. He'd noticed that difference too.

Maybe it was her freckles, dimpled chin, and gapped front teeth that made her seem vulnerable in some way? Her curly copper-colored hair was longer and darker than the last time he saw her, but her eyes were the same, a deep blue, with the sickle-shaped scar over her right eye. There were dark circles under those eyes now.

Moving back to Ree Heights after years of living in a city was no doubt a challenge for her. James knew about the adjustments a person had to make to fit into a small community where everyone knew everyone else's history. Coming back to Fort Thompson and the reservation after college was a decision he didn't regret, but he couldn't pretend it was always easy living in, and working for, a tight-knit community.

Lucas opened the bag of sandwiches. He lifted his head and said with a grin, "Just having a smell, Dad."

James laughed. "Are you getting hungry, Lucas?"

They were heading west to the rodeo and powwow grounds. Today's rodeo and dancing would be a gathering of reservation families. Most lived on remote ranches scattered across the reservation. James and Sandra had grown up on the ranch where their parents still lived.

Their parents had worked hard to make sure the family attended as many of these kinds of get-togethers as they could when James and Sandra were growing up. Those links to his heritage and culture were important to James and he wanted the same for his son.

James pulled his pickup into the line of trucks parked at the edge of rodeo grounds behind the tribal council buildings in the heart of Lower Brule.

Lucas jumped out of the truck and around to his Dad's side, pulling his hand. "Come on, Dad, let's go!"

James looked around at the gathering just getting underway. He saw blankets spread out on the grass, loaded with baskets and coolers and piles of clothes. Young and old milled around greeting friends and family. Older men with their big cowboy hats in saggy lawn chairs swapped stories. Babies slept on some of the blankets. Kids chased each other and got scolded to play out away from the blankets. Older women caught up on news and set out food on the blankets. Younger women walked with their toddlers -- holding the chubby fingers. Teenagers, male and female, tiled heads in toward their secrets. He breathed in deeply and felt his shoulders relax.

"Hey, Gramma!" Lucas ran for his grandparents, whom he had just spotted.

"Lucas, let me see you." James could hear his mom as he came up behind Lucas. "My goodness, you've grown!"

Leaving Lucas with his mom, James walked with his dad to the arena -- a large fenced area used for rodeo events. Wooden stands for the spectators ran along the side of the arena while at one end a tottering two-story tower waited for the rodeo judges and Gilbert Spotted Calf. Gilbert would emcee the dancing in the afternoon and then, later, would announce the events at the rodeo in the early evening.

At the end of the arena a cloud of dust hung above pens holding the livestock. Steers to be used in the bulldogging and roping events bawled from their pens while unbroken horses for the bronc riding event tossed their heads and circled the fences.

James and his dad leaned against the fence and scanned the livestock.

"That guy'll give somebody a run for their money." James' dad indicated one particularly snarly horse.

They stood watching for a few minutes. The horse pawed the ground, lowered his head and blew tiny drifts of dust into the air. He looked up at the men then shook his head.

His dad looked at James. "Everything OK?"

James glanced at his dad and asked. "You heard anything about AIM coming into the area?"

"Oh sure. There are rumors. Anything to liven the

boredom?" His dad chuckled.

"So you don't think there's anything to it?" James watched the horse circle around the pen. He and his dad drew back when it stormed by them.

"I don't know." His dad paused, watching the horse circle again. "Around here folks are pretty content with their lives, but there are some on other reservations who feel trapped and wronged by both the federal government and tribal government."

"I get that. Over at Rosebud and Pine Ridge." James moved back from the fence. "I'd like to think people here have more sense than to invite outsiders into their business."

James and his dad moved toward the other end of the grounds and a large grassy area. Shelters made from tree boughs placed across the top of wooden frameworks provided shade for the elders attending the festivities. Drummers, men of all ages, were seated on tree stumps or folding chairs. They warmed up their drums using long drumsticks, the ends wrapped with cotton. Their deep rhythmic thumping signaled the start of the dancing. Gilbert's booming voice called out to folks to get themselves organized for the first event, the Jingle Dress Dance.

James sat with his parents and extended family to watch the dancing while Lucas ran around with friends.

"Oh, James, look." His mom nodded toward a young woman who had just entered the dancing. She was striking in her long beaded dress and moccasins, her hair pulled up and dressed with feathers. "You remember Christine? She's moved back. Unmarried."

He snorted good-naturedly. "Thanks, Ma, but I can handle my own love life."

"Just trying to help." She chuckled.

He glanced at her and added, "Besides I have to get divorced first."

She considered for moment then asked, "I guess you haven't heard anything from Martha?"

"I haven't heard from her since just after she left." He decided not to mention the rumor of her return. "She made it pretty clear then she wouldn't divorce me unless she could have custody of Lucas. And that won't happen."

Their conversation ended abruptly when Lucas skidded to a stop in front of James. "Dad, I can stay with Granma and Granpa all week, right?" He gave his Granma a big grin.

"Ha. Yep." James replied as Lucas bounded away. He heard Lucas tell his friend. "See. I told you. I get to stay all week."

James wanted to relax with his family and enjoy the fellowship of his community, but he was distracted with a nagging worry. Could guns really be coming onto his reservation? And with them, the possibility of violence?

## Chapter 9

Vera wanted more information about Johnny. What was he doing in the area? Why had he stolen Wally's rifle? What had he wanted from her parents? What connection could he possibly have with Crow Creek?

She'd make calls tomorrow to investigate the death of

Thomas Yellow-Knife. Today she'd pay a visit to someone who might know something about Johnny's February visit to his parents. She drove slowly through town. There were no cars on the main street on a late Sunday afternoon. That felt familiar. She'd only ever known Ree Heights as a ghost of its earlier self.

Ree Heights had begun as a tank town, one of many towns lined up along the rail line every 12 miles or so across central South Dakota, strategically located so the steam-driven engines could take on water. Vera had grown up with the deserted buildings and knew bits of their stories, the implement store, the print shop, the telephone exchange, the bank converted into the post office for a generation but now shuttered. She knew that from its beginning in 1881 until the start of depression of 1930, Ree Heights had been, more or less, a prosperous town. All of her life, she had been witness to the town's continuing slide toward its slow extinction.

She parked her car behind an old building. The front of the brick building housed the store/post office while the rear of the building served as Charlotte's home. A somewhat recent transplant to the area, Charlotte served as the post mistress as well as proprietress of the general store. Charlotte and Vera's mom had been close friends and since her return to Ree Heights, Vera had begun a friendship of her own with Charlotte.

Vera saw Charlotte stretched out on a lawn chair under an impressive oak tree.

Charlotte lowered her book and gave Vera a wave.

As Vera walked up to the backyard seating she'd noticed Charlotte's toenails peeking out from her long skirt were the same red as her lipstick, matching the frames of her eyeglasses. The cat on her lap arched her back and settled again.

"Join me?" Charlotte invited her. A nearly empty glass and a plate of crumbs rested on the small table beside her.

"There's tea in the fridge," she offered, raised her eyebrows, then smiled. "Unless you'd like something stronger?"

"Thanks." Vera gave her a slow smile. "Don't mind if I do."

"There's a bottle of wine open on the counter," Charlotte

directed Vera from her comfortable seat. "Oh and there's a letter for you."

Vera returned with a glass, the bottle of wine, and the letter. She refilled Charlotte's glass then filled her own.

She sat down crosswise in a lawn chair next to Charlotte's, ripped open the envelope and quickly read through the letter from the Minneapolis Police Department. She let her hand drop and sighed deeply.

Charlotte raised her head from where it rested against the back of the seat and turned toward Vera. "What's wrong?"

"It seems that my employment with the Minneapolis Police Department has been officially terminated. When I took a leave of absence back at the end of April to come stay in Ree Heights after the accident, I was given six weeks to return. Obviously I haven't."

"Oh, I see." Charlotte responded.

Vera took a long look at her new friend. "I knew this was coming. It just feels so final."

"Vera, I'm so sorry." Charlotte sat up, a look of concern on her face.

"I mean, what am I supposed to do. I need to be here with Wally and I need to figure out what I'm going to do with the ranch." Vera turned away and blinking.

"You've had so much to contend with, Vera." Charlotte watched a trace of a tear slide down Vera's cheek.

Charlotte knew from Elsa that Vera had left Ree Heights under difficult circumstances. She was learning that Vera was a private person. She wanted to both share an awareness of Vera's feelings and avoid prying into those feelings so she let the conversation go and returned to her lounging position.

Vera spent a minute looking into the blurring bushes bordering the property, then stretched out in her chair and closed her eyes. The afternoon sun drifted gently down through the canopy of leaves, the air heavy with the scent of lilac.

Vera sighed, opened her eyes and watched a robin hop through the grass poking the ground for worms for her babies.

She wanted a break from her responsibilities. She wanted a distraction.

She rolled her head toward Charlotte. "You've lived in Ree Heights for ten years?"

Charlotte's head was resting against the back of the chair and her eyes were closed as she started her story. "I think you know that I grew up in Washington, DC. I went to college in the city and made a home there after my graduation." She glanced at Vera.

Vera turned her head and nodded. "Right."

"My family's originally from this area. I'd come out here summers to spend time with my cousins. I was a summer cousin." Charlotte smiled at the memory and continued. "After my second divorce and with a pending shake-up in the mortgage company where I worked, I decided I was ready for a change. I moved to Ree Heights for what I thought would be a year or so but yes, ten years later, I'm still here."

"Don't you miss the city? Doesn't the smallness drive you

crazy sometimes?"

"It does, at times." Charlotte chuckled. "But the other qualities of the community and the people who live here have come to matter more to me.

"What about you, Vera? I know why you are here now." She sat up to refill their glasses. "Tell me about what you've left behind."

Some of her stress, and the rest of the afternoon, slipped away while Vera shared with Charlotte the major points of her life in Minneapolis. About how, after completing her degree in Criminal Justice from South Dakota State University, she moved to Minneapolis. About how the fast pace of life took some getting used to, but how she'd gradually acclimated to the city's vibrancy. About how theaters, bars, libraries, and corner cafes had become enmeshed in her daily routine.

Vera talked about working her way up the ladder in the Minneapolis Police Department. How it had been educational, eye-opening, and, at times, difficult. Women cops were few and far between when she started on the force. She'd had to work hard to earn the respect of her male colleagues. She eventually landed a position in the Domestic Violence Division. In the years with that division, Vera explained, she and her colleagues developed a novel approach to domestic abuse, using a cooling-off period followed by mediation for those people involved in the conflict. The new protocols were getting national attention.

"Sounds like meaningful work, Vera." Charlotte was sitting up and had turned in her chair to follow Vera's story. "I can imagine that it's been hard to be away from it. It feels like you are missing out?"

"Well, yeah, it's been hard to be away." She had grown quiet, remembering an especially hostile husband she had arrested last winter. He had waited for her outside the station late one night and followed her back to her apartment. It'd been a frigid night in January. While she fumbled for her key in the dark entrance, he'd come up from behind her. She fought him as his hands tightened around neck. He'd screamed his wrath, about her messing with his family. She defended herself with a knee into his groin and escaped into her apartment.

She shook off her memories and gave Charlotte a half-smile. "But there are some things I'm not missing."

Charlotte drained the last of the wine from the bottle into their glasses and asked. "Anyone special you've left behind?"

As Charlotte relaxed back into her chair, the cat, which had earlier jumped off her lap, leaped back onto its spot.

Vera rested her head against the back of the chair. "I do have a boyfriend, Simon. We've dated for three years but honestly I'm not sure our relationship is based on much more than convenience?"

Vera finished the wine in her glass, then swung her feet around to the ground.

"Someone walked into Wally's shop this morning and walked off with one of his rifles." She scowled, remembering.

"What? You're kidding." Charlotte pulled herself up, looking shocked. "In broad daylight? In Miller?"

With Charlotte's sudden movement, the cat had jumped out of the cozy lap.

Vera furrowed her eyes and asked. "Charlotte, did you ever know Johnny Larson?"

Charlotte studied Vera thoughtfully. "No, though your Mom has mentioned him to me."

Charlotte looked puzzled. "Why do you ask?"

"He was at my place early this morning helping himself to gas." Vera shook her head and growled. "And I'm pretty sure it was Johnny who stole Wally's rifle."

Charlotte looked confused. "You think it was Johnny?"

"He's up to something." Vera was frowning. "He gave me a sort of cryptic warning this morning. Something about the less I know, the better."

Vera sat for a minute, then asked, "Did Mom ever say anything to you about Johnny? I know he was a friend of Dad's. I remember his showing up at our house years ago in a bush plane. I was only ten or eleven at the time. He told us wild stories about flying into exotic places with shipments of guns. I'm not sure Mom really approved of him."

Charlotte picked up the glass of wine to take a sip, realized it was empty, then set it back down. "Oh, well yes, from what she'd said, her relationship with Johnny was a bit complicated."

Charlotte rearranged her skirt. "Maybe you didn't know that Elsa and Johnny had dated, just before she and your dad got together?"

"Really?" Vera looked intently at Charlotte who was looking into the yard. "I never knew Mom had dated Johnny. Wonder why she never told me?"

Charlotte glanced at Vera. "Everett was gone out of the area, serving in the war. Elsa and Johnny were a year behind Everett in school."

Charlotte paused for a moment then went on. "Elsa was young. There was so much uncertainty what with the war. About how long it might drag on. Everett hadn't promised her anything. She wasn't sure if or when she would see him again."

Vera leaned forward, listening intently.

Charlotte again glanced at Vera before adding. "Everett's tour ended abruptly when he was released on medical discharge."

"Right," Vera interrupted. "He had a ruptured appendix. He only served in the Navy for one year."

Charlotte continued with the story. "Well, when your dad got back to the area, he made his feelings known to your mom, that he wanted to renew their romance."

"They married a month after dad came back. I've heard this story." Vera knew her tone sounded sharp.

Charlotte finished the story. "Johnny left the area soon after your parents were married."

The branches of the oak tree above were filled with bird song and fluttering.

After a minute, Vera pushed herself out of the chair. "Thanks for the wine and the conversation, Charlotte."

"Anytime Vera." The cat was back in Charlotte's lap -- curled up and sleeping.

Vera drove away feeling oddly unsettled.

## Chapter 10

The old pickup was throwing up dust as Johnny pointed it to an out of the way spot he knew of. He needed some time to think about what to do next. He felt numb. Confused. He'd only known Thomas a few months. Their future had been cut short.

He was sorry to have stolen Wally's rifle but he needed a weapon. He needed to arm himself for his next move though he wasn't sure what that would be. Ironic, he thought, he knew where there were a lot of weapons but he couldn't get to them just now.

His partners were unlikely to remain patient for much longer. They would want to complete the deal with the radicals from the reservation and get out of the state.

He'd come up to the area a few months ago when he'd heard that there might be a market for his goods. That was the first time he'd met Thomas and the last time he saw Everett and

Elsa.

When he had settled in Denver after being forced out of a career of flying mercenary missions into warring countries, he found a niche market for the services and skills he had spent his adult life cultivating.

He had set up a contract with AIM to deliver rifles to the Crow Creek reservation. He knew the rifles would be headed into the hands of those who wanted to change no matter the cost. That was the sort of clientele he had dealt with throughout his career. He knew the history of the treatment meted out by the U.S. government to Native tribes. He couldn't blame them if they wanted to blow the entire reservation apart.

It was his policy to never let himself get involved in the motives of his customers. His usual approach to this business was to deliver the black market goods and never look back. He had doubted that a group of malcontents out on the reservation could get organized enough with money enough to follow through with the contract.

But so much was turning out differently than he anticipated.

## Chapter 11

The phone was ringing when Vera walked into the house. She hurried to pick it up, the dogs on her heels.

"This is Albert Phinney."

"Hi, Albert. I didn't expect to hear from you so soon."

"I'm calling to let you know I have a preliminary finding. I'll send samples from the contents of the deceased's stomach tomorrow to Sioux Falls to be processed. Those toxicology reports won't be ready for another week or more."

"But you have an idea of how he died?"

"Yes, I have a working theory. You may let the family know the body can be released on Tuesday morning. I am aware of the tribal custom for a quick burial."

"Thanks, Albert, I'll get word to the family and come by tomorrow to talk with you." Vera waited for a response. Not hearing one, she hung up.

She dialed James' number.

A warm female voice answered the phone. "James isn't here just now. Can I take a message?"

She stumbled on her reply. "Oh thanks. Would you let him know Vera called?"

She set the phone down, feeling worn out from the roller coaster day.


## Chapter 12

After supper Vera moved out onto the front porch and into the swing her dad had hung up for her mom years ago. A nearly full moon was rising over the barn at the far end of yard, bright, tinged with orange. Clouds were building along the edges of the horizon.

In the deepening twilight, Vera could hear bats out in the yard squeaking as they flew through the warm, humid atmosphere finding their dinner. Their shadows flitted in and out of the beam of light streaming from a bulb mounted on a pole out in the barnyard.

The dogs were sprawled out, their limbs twitching in their dreams. The ever-present wind had tempered to a breeze. Vera breathed in the coolness of the enveloping darkness.

She pushed back in the swing and recalled Johnny's visit nearly twenty years ago when he had shown up on a late afternoon in early August. He had landed his small plane on the blacktop then taxied up the gravel driveway, hopped out of the Cessna 170 taildragger and walked up to the house, ready for some conversation.

She remembered Johnny as handsome and full of energy. He had leaned back in a kitchen chair, warming up to his story. "I wasn't getting paid enough to fly the operations under our government so I had to jump ship."

"Who you workin for now, Johnny?" her dad had asked, sipping his drink. He'd come in out of the fields early, ready to knock off for the day, and ready for the entertaining diversion

Johnny's visit could offer to his daily routine.

Vera remembered that she'd hung on the adult conversation, captivated by the details of the exotic locales.

"Algerians, South Vietnam, insurgents in Central America. Whoever pays the most," Johnny had boasted. "Flying in guns the U.S. government is willing to sell but doesn't want to be linked to." No doubt he had been embellishing his narrative for his audience, she thought now, as an adult.

Johnny had taken a slow sip of his drink. "In Algeria I was commissioned to fly in munitions for the National Liberation Front. I landed my cargo plane under the cover of night in the mountains to the west of the main city, Algiers. It was a hand-dug landing strip lighted with lanterns set along the course." He paused for effect, then continued with his story. "I set that big boy down with a landing that nearly jarred the teeth out of my head and got to a stop with just a couple of feet to spare. Fighters appeared outta nowhere that night and took possession of the goods I had flown in. Got paid in French francs and Algerian dinar." Johnny chuckled a little and pulled the coins from his pocket to show them. He gave her one of the coins to keep. "The French-backed government had more than they could handle when the NLF guerrillas got ahold of the guns I delivered to them."

Her dad had pushed back with his response. "Sounds dangerous? What do you do if you're shot down?"

"I won't be." Johnny blustered. "Plus I've got government ties to connect me with people who can get me out of trouble if it comes to that."

It was late evening when Johnny suggested a next adventure. "So Everett, I got a tip on a beautiful spread in southern Manitoba. Sounds like the owners are desperate to sell. What do ya say, we take a little trip up north and take a look?"

By noon the next day, her Dad was in the plane with Johnny headed for Canada. There was a ranch for sale south of Winnipeg. Vera thought now of her dad as an eternal optimist. His tolerance for risk was one characteristic of his unrealistic hopefulness. Perhaps a necessary trait in the dramatic ups and downs of ranching?

They were gone through that weekend, showing back up on Monday near the end of the day. Johnny didn't come into the house. He dropped Everett off, then taxied his bush plane down the driveway and up onto the paved valley road. He caught a tailwind and was gone.

Vera hadn't seen him again -- until today.


## Chapter 13

The dogs jumped to their feet when Vera stood up, thinking to follow her into the house.

"You two stay. It's cooler out here."

They plopped back down on the porch.

She walked into the dark kitchen, pulled on the string for the light above the counter, and ran hot water in the kitchen sink to wash dishes that had piled up. Her thoughts moved to James and the surprise encounter with him.

They had first met in the spring of their senior year of high school at a conference on Criminal Justice held at Black Hills State College. It had felt so liberating to be away from home and on her own, Vera remembered. Meeting James had been liberating too. A declaration of independence. They had begun a relationship that spring in the Hills and continued it through the summer. Or tried to.

Tracking the activities of each person in the area, and commenting on them, is the main form of entertainment in a small town. At the core of the behavior is a fear of change. All members of the small and closed community are expected to follow a prescribed set of rules. These rules check, and curb, behaviors that fall outside the accepted norms. The rules are meant to keep the members safe and secure. The price for that security is an intolerance for any activity, person, event or ideas that seem to threaten the security.

Vera glanced at her somber reflection in the dark steamy window above the sink. Just because she now better understood the group behavior, thanks to a first-year college course in Psychology, didn't mean she could accept it.

Dating James that summer years ago brought out some unpleasant and even ugly truths about her hometown. At first, she had been surprised, but thought little of the shunning she received, though it was disconcerting to have the conversation grind to a complete halt when she walked up to a group of friends. She could have lived with that level of criticism, but things began to escalate as the summer wore on. First there was the message scrawled on the window of her car. "Stay away from the Indian." Nothing too subtle about that. She couldn't imagine that there could be anyone in her community so bigoted and spiteful.

She remembered she'd asked James if he was getting any pushback from people in his community about our relationship. He had looked puzzled and wondered why anyone would care?

The final incident that convinced her to give up on their relationship came at the end of July. Her dad had gone out to check his cows one morning and found a neighbor's bull in with his herd. Someone had cut the barb wire fence and had left a note secured to the barbwire fence. "Got a problem with the invading bull?" Her dad was hot, ready to get the Sheriff involved, but her mom had talked him down. She reminded him that they lived in a small town with people they had to rely on and that it was unlikely that there would be any way to figure out who had done it. Best just to leave it alone.

She hadn't told James all of what had happened. Somehow it was too painful and embarrassing. She had felt confused and betrayed by the reactions from those whom she had always felt warmth and caring. Thinking about it now, she knew that those feelings of distrust and disappointment that had pushed her away had not disappeared from her memory.

Vera stood at the window and wondered if now, with more life experience, she could have handled the situation differently.

A slight breeze moved through the open window. The noises of the day had given way to the hushed sounds of nighttime. She could hear crickets in the grass, the chirps of raccoons down near the creek, and the sounds of cows calling to their calves. There was a faint smell of skunk in the air.

## Chapter 14

Johnny stumbled into the cold interior of the old structure and waited for his sight to adjust to the darkness. With the moonlight streaming through the broken windows he stepped carefully through the space, hearing the scratching of escaping rodents.

God, he had so many memories of this old hall. He and Elsa had come up to dances held in the Grange in the year before Everett came home from Japan.

Johnny and Everett had been best friends growing up in Ree Heights, Everett a year older than Johnny. When Everett joined the Army, he had entrusted Elsa, his girlfriend, to Johnny. Everett's early return had been a surprise to both Elsa and Johnny.

His footsteps sounded hollow as he moved through the cavernous room and up onto the low stage where the bands had once set up for the dances. As his vision became accustomed to the gloom, he saw he wasn't the first to take refuge in the abandoned building. Old blankets and clothing littered the floor.

He pushed the castoff remnants together, lowered himself to the pile, then pulled out a bottle and took a long pull. The liquor burned his throat. He could feel the alcohol travel to his stomach then out to his limbs, warming him as it moved through his body.

When he was in Fort Thompson at the end of February, he had finally made contact with Thomas. He hadn't expected to be so moved with the experience of meeting the boy. He had learned he had a son when he moved back to Denver two years before. He hadn't been convinced a relationship with the boy was something he wanted.

When Johnny had picked up Thomas from his aunt's house that first time in February, Thomas had brought along a map of the United States.

"Let's drive over to the river." Thomas directed Johnny to a stretch of the Missouri where the river made a deep oxtail bend. There was a large wetlands of standing cattails and bunched grasses, bent, frozen and brown. As he unfolded the map he'd brought along, Thomas began to describe the migratory route of the whooping crane. Johnny could see the route marked in red on the map.

"The cranes move from southern Texas in late March to their summer home in Canada." Thomas was pointing to the ice encrusted edges of the wide slough. "They stop here to rest."

Johnny couldn't remember much about Thomas' mother, Susan. They had spent a few months together in Denver one summer nineteen years ago. He had been between jobs; she had just moved to the city. Because they were both from the same area in South Dakota, they'd felt a bond.

He left Denver in October of that year headed for Southeast Asia to deliver munitions to the Vietnamese in their fight against the French colonial government. He hadn't given much more thought to Susan.

When he resettled in Denver and chanced to run into an old friend, he learned Susan had been pregnant when he left all those years ago. He also learned that Susan had died in a car accident when their son was two years old. Thomas had been sent to live with her aunt.

His friend had stayed in touch with Thomas over the years and was able to let Johnny know how to find his son. The friend said Thomas knew Johnny was his father and was curious to meet him.

Snippets of conversation with Thomas, along with scenes from their hours together, pinged through his mind as Johnny lay on the dusty floor in the shadowy darkness, sipping from the bottle.

As they sat in the car and watched the river flow past, Thomas talked about high school and how he loved to play basketball.

"I may not be so tall but I'm quick and I'm a good shot," he said with a grin. "Coach can count on me for baskets from the free throw line."

Thomas was excited for his upcoming graduation.

"I want to study biology. Eventually." He glanced at Johnny. "When I get enough money together to go to the university."

Thomas continued laying out his plan. "First, though, I'll get training in welding or a trade so I can earn better money and be able to save up for college."

The moonlight slanted through the high windows. Johnny tried to get comfortable on the hard floor, using his rolled up coat as a pillow. He could hear mice racing along the floorboards and could smell their scent along with all manner of other odors -- decaying wood, musty and molding fabric, and urine.

Thinking of Thomas now, he almost couldn't believe he could be his father. Thomas was all that was good, responsible, and kind.

"I work out at a ranch just north of town," Thomas had told him. "I'm helping Franklin with the calving now and will be living out there through the summer. I can work the hay fields and give him a hand with chores."

Thomas' chest puffed out slightly. "I can help my auntie with the money I'm making."

Johnny pulled himself up in order to lean back on the wall. He stared out into the empty dark space. God, why had he waited two years to reach out to Thomas?

Eventually, their conversation turned to Susan. Thomas couldn't remember much about her and Johnny couldn't provide many details for him.

In the dim milky light he could just make out his son's face in the small school photo. He looked to be about twelve years old. Thomas had given it to him on their second meeting that weekend in February.

"Thought you might like a picture of me." Thomas had glanced at Johnny and slowly pulled the picture from his pocket.

Johnny took the picture, held it for a few quiet moments then suggested Thomas could come to live with him in Denver in the fall and attend a community college there. Johnny had surprised himself with the suggestion.

Thomas had jumped on the idea. Johnny asked Thomas if he might want to live with him while he attended school. Thomas thought that would be great. They approached their new relationship shyly, tentatively, hopefully. Both of them sensing a void that the other could fill.

Johnny squeezed his eyes shut and moaned.

He had left Thomas, there in the barn. Dead.

His thoughts continued to arise restlessly and unbidden. He'd been on the other side of death for most of his adult life, had provided the means for killing. Now inside twenty-four hours, the three people who meant the most to him were dead.

He drained the bottle of liquor and wiggled around, trying to find a more agreeable position.

## Chapter 15

The pungent smell of the central Nebraska wetlands swept through the open windows of the car. Randall had started the drive from Denver in the late afternoon and now was traveling through rolling sand hills that stretched for a hundred miles unbroken by any towns and virtually no traffic. The calls of the red-winged blackbirds as they settled in the cattails for the night served to soothe his spirit.

A full moon shining on the undulating countryside allowed his mind to drift and reflect on his past and on his plans for the future.

He moved off Crow Creek reservation with his mom when he was young. She often said that there was no future for her or her kids on the rez. Their father was either dead or gone -- he could never get a straight answer out of her.

Being the oldest of the three kids, Randall remembered the first months of living on Denver's northwest side. They moved mid-winter into a two room unfurnished apartment -- something they could almost afford. His mom needed to find a job quick. He remembered the worry stretched across her face.

They slept huddled together on a couple of mattresses on the floor. He'd been ten years old that winter, his two sisters, six and four. His mom found a job waiting tables at the IHOP two bus stops from their apartment. He took care of his sisters so didn't get to school for the rest of that year.

Eventually they met other Natives in the neighborhood and while their life in the city was never easy, they did manage to survive. Randall spent more time out of school than in and eventually dropped out. He figured he had gotten enough of what the white school system had to offer.

As a teenager he gained his footing in a local gang. They were loyal to each other, for a time, until fighting over lovers and drugs, pregnancies, and police arrests broke up their fellowship. Jail time had reduced the group considerably. White cops in the city had it in for them.

Randall grew up hearing his mom's stories of how life had been for his people in the old days. How the tribe had worked together for the welfare of all. How each person was vital to the whole. How they roamed over the plains hunting buffalo and raising their families in the traditional way.

He had been back to the Crow Creek reservation a few times in his younger years, enough to know that a traditional lifestyle was a thing of the past for Natives. Whites had taken away their lands, their traditions, and their language. The white government lied to them time and time again. Nothing that came out of Washington could be trusted.

Randall understood his mother's desire to provide a better life for herself and her kids. He intended to do the same, now, for his people. But in a different way. He would help bring change to the reservation.

Randall slowed the old car as he came into Valentine, looking for a gas station. Shit, nothing open this late. Only forty miles to the Rosebud reservation and the town of Mission where he had friends.

Nothing to do but wait til morning.

He parked behind a truck stop, rolled up the windows to keep the mosquitoes out, and tried to get comfortable. His thoughts moved to the past again and one of the last times he'd been on the Crow Creek reservation.

Randall remembered one of the last times he had gone with his mom and sisters to visit family and friends in Fort Thompson. He'd been twelve or thirteen at the time. They had stayed with relatives and were in and out of homes for dinners and ceremonies. Even then the reservation life had seemed like a dead end to Randall. As he got older, he couldn't figure out why so many on the reservation seemed satisfied with their lives. He could never understand their complacency. It was as if they didn't know their own history. As if they didn't realize what they had lost.

In the past couple of years, Randall had met up with plenty of Natives from the Pine Ridge and Rosebud reservations who thought the way he did. Young men and women who had moved to the city but who were committed to fight for change back on their homelands. They were angry about the disrespect and disregard by the white government. Over the years the promises from the government in Washington had rolled through the reservations like so many tumbleweeds. They couldn't be trusted. Some on the reservation found power in a relationship with the federal government. It was just wrong that some in the tribal governments were in cahoots with the Bureau of Indian Affairs. Wrong that Natives would side with the Feds against their own people. Randall and his friends intended to end that relationship.

Randall had made contact with American Indian Movement. He saw his chance to make a difference for his people. He let the AIM leadership know he had the connections to secure weapons from the black market. They had come up with the money. It'd taken a few months to get the deal set up. Now it was a matter of putting all the pieces together.

He leaned his back against the door and stretched out as best he could, closed his eyes, and listened to the yelping of coyotes running and hunting along the bluffs above the nearby Niobrara river.

## *Chapter 16*

Still sticky with the day's treats, Lucas had fallen asleep almost immediately after James tucked him into the trundle bed in his old room at his parents' house. They had stayed through the dancing in the afternoon and later watched the rodeo, getting back to the ranch just after dark.

James sat with his parents at the kitchen table for a few minutes drinking coffee before making his way out to his truck for the drive back to town. They chuckled over how Lucas had moved in a small posse of friends during the day. The boys had run and played and danced -- and eaten at the picnic sites of many families.

Windows rolled down, James drove through the light of a low-slung, but ripening moon. The road leading out of the ranch property followed a dry creek bed lined with massive cottonwood trees. James had always thought that if those cottonwoods could talk, they could share a lot of the history of the area and its inhabitants.

Life had never been easy for the Native populations living on the prairie. The Arikara and Mandan tribes that had farmed along the Missouri River were nearly wiped out with diseases in the late 1700s.

His ancestors, the Sioux, who came next to occupy the grasslands of the high plains, rode in on horseback from neighboring states. The tribes moved across the prairie, following the herds of bison.

In the 1860s, in an attempt to control the tribes, the U.S. government instituted the policy of killing off the bison to near

96

extinction. It had the desired effect. Without the lifeblood of the buffalo, the tribes were more easily corralled onto reservations and at the mercy of the federal government.

Hard times were a common thread in their history. Perseverance and community were the backbone of their story of survival.

The bright light of the full moon illuminated the landscape. Looking out across the prairie, he saw antelope in the distance. They lifted their heads for a moment then returned to grazing.

James let the sights and sounds of the powwow and rodeo move through his mind as he drove. He smiled, remembering his mom calling attention to a childhood friend of his participating in one of the dances. He hadn't meant to be so sharp in his reply to her.

God knows, he'd like to end his relationship with his wife. Maybe, if the rumors were true, Martha might be making an appearance on the reservation and he could finally serve her with divorce papers. His neck and shoulders tightened as he leaned forward over the steering wheel. There was no way he would let her get her hands on Lucas.

The dirt roads, rutted from spring rains, forced James to slow down and focus in order to keep his tires out of the deep troughs. He let out a long breath and leaned back in the seat.

His thumb tapped the steering wheel and his brows pulled together as he thought about the gossip he had heard today at the gathering. It was talk of unrest -- more than unrest -- outright rebellion -- gathering steam on the neighboring reservations of Pine Ridge and Rosebud. It all fit with what he'd heard from Sandra earlier.

Whereas there had never been a booming economy on the reservations, younger people were finding fewer opportunities for employment and therefore struggled to achieve a comfortable lifestyle. He knew they felt left out to some degree, marginalized in the community.

Building homes and families in the area, their parents and grandparents had found employment as ranchers and merchants, teachers and health care workers. Those generations had carved out peaceful and somewhat prosperous lives for themselves. Creating community in the small towns on and around the reservations, they had a strong interest in preserving their current lifestyle and they held tightly to their positions of power in the tribal government.

He worried that AIM and the violence that followed in its wake could spill over into Crow Creek. He no longer trusted that he knew the community as well as he had thought.

As it often happened, James could smell the Missouri River before he could see it. The dark bridge came into dim view. He carefully steered his pickup, with a bump, onto the structure and drove slowly across. The bright light from the moon created shadows in the black currents as the river moved swiftly and silently downstream. Looking down the beach, James saw a single light in a cabin window a quarter mile away. Must be somebody out fishing.

## Chapter 17

"I'm telling ya, man, I wasn't followed." William was late arriving.

"I snuck out of my house. My car was parked over at the church parking lot."

He pushed past Leonard, took a beer from the six-pack on the floor, opened and drank deeply. He let out a satisfied burp and asked. "When did ya say Randall was coming?"

"Don't know. Tonight maybe?" Leonard popped a can and sucked off the foam.

William gulped down the rest of his can and reached for another. "Damn. We're going to see some action after Randall gets here to buy guns from that dealer and AIM shows up."

William was ready for some excitement. He had graduated from high school a year ago. Though he had intended to go to college or at least move off to find a good job, so far none of that had happened. He still lived with his parents and sister and worked at a convenience store.

Leonard was on his feet standing at the entrance of the fishing shack located on the west bank of the Missouri River. He saw a single vehicle crossing the bridge a quarter mile away but nothing else.

Leonard turned from his lookout in the doorway. "You better keep your mouth shut about the guns and AIM?"

He was sick of this small town. He had come to Fort Thompson to hide out for awhile. Avoiding the law in southern California. That was a year ago. It felt like a lifetime.

After a few minutes of quiet, William asked. "Is it true Martha's coming back to the reservation? Heard she was hooked up with one of the AIM leaders?"

"Don't you worry about Martha. If she comes back, it'll be to get her boy." His cousin Martha had shown up in east LA about the same time he needed to get out. She stayed in

California while he moved to Fort Thompson to live with their elderly grandparents and tried to blend in. Like she'd told him to, he'd kept an eye on her son and the boy's father, a tribal police officer. He thought it damned ironic that Martha had married James. Martha was cut from the same cloth as himself. She no more wanted to settle down in this town than he did.

They waited another hour until the beer was gone. William stepped out of the cabin and walked a short way along the river's edge to relieve himself. He could see across the width of the river to the bank on the other side, dark in the shadows cast by the bright moonlight. As he stood in the mud of the river he felt the cold air coming off the water and heard the occasional plop of a fish. He yawned and walked back.

"How long're we going to wait for Randall?" William asked when he came back into the cabin. He didn't want to be a whiner but he had to get up early to go into the store.

"Shit. I guess he's not coming." Leonard threw his empty can onto a growing pile in the corner. William followed him out of the cabin.

Leonard pulled the door closed and fastened the lock.


## Chapter 18

The phone was ringing.

"This better be good," Vera growled.

She switched on a lamp and padded downstairs to answer it.

"Hey Vera, it's me."

"Simon, what are you doing calling so late?" She glanced at the clock on the wall. Well, maybe it wasn't all that late, but it had been a long day.

"Oh baby, sorry, did I wake you?" He was slurring his words. "I'm missing you."

"Sounds like you've been out tonight?" Vera wondered who of her neighbors might be listening in on this conversation.

"Yeah, went out with some of the boys. Had a few drinks." There was a pause on his end. "When ya coming back, Vera?"

Vera sucked in a big breath and let it out slowly. "Simon, I told you. I need stay here for a few months, to get things settled. Wally needs me here for a while longer."

"But I need you, Vera." Simon whined. "Baby, I'm getting tired of waiting."

"I'm sure it's hard for you, Simon." She rolled her eyes. "I'll call you in a few days?"

She heard a faint click and the line went dead.


## *Chapter 19* -- Monday morning

Coffee is a verb in Ree Heights. Farmers and ranchers drive into town to join their town neighbors most every morning to coffee and exchange news. Vera parked her VW in front of the Ree Heights Cafe, darted through the light drizzle and opened the door to the smells of coffee and bacon.

She pulled off her cowboy hat, an old one of her dad's, and knocked it against her knee to shake off the moisture. She had braided her curling hair, wanting to control the effects of the humidity.

"Mornin, Vera. Ya get some rain out at your place?" Bert scooched his chair over to make room for her at the big table in the crowded room.

From the table she heard. "Hey, Vera, that little car of yours appears to be holding up. Heard you rear-ended a deer last week?"

"Ha! That right, Vera? "

"Yep." She laughed. "All true. The deer got away. No damages. But my car needed a little work. Still runs fine though even if it's not as pretty."

She walked over to the big coffee urn behind the counter and poured herself a cup.

Erlene, the proprietress, gave her a good morning wink while she fried eggs at the big gas stove.

Down at the far end of the long counter that stretched the length of the steamy, smoky room, old Jim Ramey was sucking on a pipe and rolling dice with another ancient, Harvey Brock. The dice game would determine who would buy the other's 10 cent cup of coffee. Erlene was a good soul, she thought, letting them spend their mornings drinking up her coffee.

Carefully, with her coffee mug full to the brim, Vera pulled out a chair and settled in between Bert and Leona.

"How ya doing, gal?" her aunt asked. "How's Wally doing?"

"He's doing OK. How're things with you, Leona?" This was not the place or time to fill Leona in on Wally's stolen gun or her suspicions about the thief.

Vera sipped her coffee and looked around the big table. Older folks for the most part, people who had been born and raised in the area, and who'd never left.

The flow of the conversation was lively and informational.

First, there was the weather report.

"We got 2 tenths out at our place. Most of it come in early this morning."

"Heard Gottlieb Pietz got hail just north of his place. No damage."

"Looks like it's clearing."

"Too bad, cause we need some moisture. We're a little behind for this time of the year."

Then the livestock report.

Elmer leaned back in his chair and announced. "Saw two of Butch's cattle in Mabel Moody's garden when I drove in this morning."

"I'd say those cows are desperate. Can't say I've seen much to eat in Mabel's garden."

Some snickering.

"I'll stop by Butch's place on my way home."

Next, news of community members past and present.

"Heard Wanda, Wayne Johnson's oldest girl, has decided to take a job in Pierre."

"Word is she's planning on sharing an apartment with a friend she met in her hair training school."

"Hope she can fit into city life."

Vera hid her smile in her coffee cup. Pierre had a population of maybe 3,000.

Finally, the conversation circled around to the death down at Hasarts' place yesterday. Faces turned to Vera.

"Vera, what do you know about that Indian boy's death?"

"Heard he was working over to Franklin's this summer?"

"Heard he was a good worker."

"Franklin and Wilma pretty shook up, are they?"

"How'd he die anyway?"

"You working with the Indians on this?"

Vera talked generally about the facts of the discovered body then asked, "Has anybody seen an old blue Ford in the vicinity in the past few days."

It was quiet.

"This blue pickup has some connection in the boy's death, Vera?"

Vera was careful. "No. I'm not saying that. Just looking for the occupant who might know something."

"Don't recall that I have. But I'll give ya call if I do."

This remark was echoed by others around the table.

Though nobody present had seen Johnny's pickup, Vera suspected that by the end of the morning, she might hear from someone who knew of someone who had.

At the end of the coffee hour, Vera walked out with Carl, an old friend of her dad's and of Johnny's. Carl and her dad had settled down in Ree Heights after high school and a stint in the Army for her dad, while Johnny had departed for parts unknown.

"Everything going OK for ya, Vera?" Carl asked as they moved away from the group exiting the cafe.

"Oh yeah. Things're fine." She wasn't feeling a need to go into the details of her life just now.

Carl wore a stained ball cap pulled down over his eyes. His boots were fraying along the edges. Noticing the small holes in the jeans jacket he wore, Vera figured Carl'd been sharpening the sickles on his field mower. Her Dad's clothing used to carry similar remnants of welder sparks landing and burning the cloth.

"Looks like the alfalfa is almost ready for a first cutting?" she asked as they walked to his truck.

The rain had ended. The clouds were lifting and the day was starting to heat up. Vera could feel the humidity rise as it steamed off the asphalt.

When they were safely out of earshot of others, she turned to him. "Carl, I'm wondering, have you heard anything from Johnny Larson lately?"

He glanced at her intense expression, then pulled on the brim of the cap and rubbed it up and down on his forehead. "Well, ya know, last I heard, Johnny was located in Colorado, the Denver area."

"Oh yeah?" She was studying his face.

"He gave me a call a couple of years back, wanting to borrow some money. Said he was in some hot water with creditors." Carl cleared his throat and looked away. "But I guess you know how ranching's been going."

She knew many ranchers and farmers in the area had gone out of business in recent years -- foreclosed on by the banks when they couldn't pay on their loans.

"Ya think he asked Dad for money?" Vera didn't know if her dad would have been able to turn him down if Johnny had asked him.

"He might've." He looked at Vera for a long moment. "But it's not likely Everett and Elsa had any money to loan him either."

"Right." She nodded and looked back at the coffee klatch dispersing. She found herself again regretting the little connection she had had with her parents and brother in the past few years.

Carl turned to his pickup and got in. It was losing paint in parts. The back fender had been poached from a different vehicle. The grill covering the front of the truck was rusting.

"Why ya asking about Johnny?" He asked through the open window, his elbow resting on the doorframe.

"He came by the place yesterday." Vera looked up at Carl's

weathered face. "Looking ragged and acting mysterious."

"Is that right?" Carl frowned.

Carl looked out through the front window then back at her. "I'll keep a look out for him."

He pulled his cap back down low on his forehead and gave her a long look. "Vera, you take care now."

He started his truck, and drove away.

Talking with Carl had sparked an idea.

She got in her Bug and headed north.

Vera parked in front of the old building, shut off the motor and listened to the sounds of birds in the nearby trees. Parts of the roof had caved in and many of its windows were broken out. The heavy double doors in the front hung open.

Before its demise, the Cedar Grange had been the heart of a small prairie community with the association providing much needed social interactions for the families of farmers and ranchers living in that area, especially in the years before telephones and dependable roads.

Vera knew some of the history of the Grange Movement, how it began after the Civil War as a way to organize farmers around shared economic concerns and to educate them in new agricultural practices.

A bird flew out over her head as she made her way carefully through the entrance and up the steps into the large main room. In the dim light she could see the raised stage at the end of room. Though eerily quiet now, she could imagine the vitality of the past. Bands had played at the Cedar Grange in the years before and during World War II.

She had grown up hearing stories about how young men and women from Ree Heights would head up to the hall to dance and drink, out of sight from their families and neighbors. She could relate with the feelings Johnny and Carl and her parents might have had in wanting to slip away from the bounds of small town conventions for a few hours of freedom.

Dust motes drifted in the daylight passing through the window openings. She walked up the steps to the old stage. It seemed evident that, if not Johnny, others had taken refuge in the old building. Poking around the jumble of clothing and bedding on the floor of the space, she found a photo of a young boy, unrecognizable in the dim light. She slipped it into her back pocket.

Vera shielded her eyes as she came out of the dusty darkness into the bright morning sun and looked around. She stirred through an old campfire behind the building, uncovering animal bones and an old Jack Daniels bottle in the ashes. Rusting beer cans littered the weeds and bits of trash were caught in the scruffy grass. From the corner of her eye, she saw a flash of white.

Standing up slowly and moving back carefully, she tried to see through the shelterbelt of trees. Suddenly, with its tail up, a white-tailed deer leapt over the wire fence encircling the old property.

Letting out her breath, she walked back to her car and headed home.

A worry was taking shape in her mind. If Johnny were on

the run, who was after him? What kind of danger did they pose to the community?

## Chapter 20

Johnny drove with his windows down. The cab filled with a refreshing coolness along with the scent of rain from the night before. He watched clouds scuttling across the morning sky, pushed along by the ever-present South Dakota wind. He was headed to Kadoka, a town just off Interstate 90, and his partners. He knew his delayed return was going to be a problem.

Kadoka had seen a better day. Wall Drug signs pointed travelers to the tourist attraction 100 miles west. He dodged potholes and passed boarded up buildings on his way to the broken-down Vision Quest Motel.

Paint had long since peeled off the sign and the awning over the front office sagged heavily at one corner. Grass and weeds grew up through the cracks in the parking area and sidewalks in front of the rooms.

Johnny drove his truck to the end of the long cantaloupe-colored rectangular building, parked, and sat for a minute before he climbed out.

He leaned the stolen rifle along the side of the building out of sight, then moved to the door.

The curtains were closed.

Over the rumble of interstate truck traffic a half mile away, he could hear the sounds of the television and male voices.

He knocked. A large balding man cracked open the door.

His association with Vince Blazo and Bobby Durant had begun nearly a year and half ago. After moving back to Denver, Johnny lived large, buying expensive cars and lavishly entertaining new acquaintances he wanted to impress. In a few months he had burned through his own money and was heavily in debt. Faced with angry creditors, he found it expedient to return to his career of twenty years, the buying and selling of weapons.

Early in his new business venture, he crossed paths with

Vince and Bobby.

Their combined skill sets helped cement their loose partnership. Vince and Bobby had the contacts with those wanting black market guns and Johnny had the connections to the weapons.

Because he'd grown up in the area and knew his way around, Johnny was the leader in the forthcoming transaction on the reservation, an arrangement that didn't make his partners very happy.

"Git in here." A meaty hand grabbed Johnny's shirt front and pulled him into the darkened room.

The door slammed behind him. Light coming from the TV illuminated the unmade beds, ashtrays overflowing with cigarette butts, and empty beer cans littering nearly every surface. The room reeked of unwashed bodies, booze, and smoke.

"Where the hell've you been?" Vince shoved Johnny toward the door. "You take off on Saturday night and show up now?"

Though his body was going soft in the middle and along

his jowls, Vince was strong and deadly with a knife. And quick to anger. Johnny had once seen Vince cut a punk in an argument over an overdue payment. Ending the discussion, Vince had sliced open the kid's cheek. It would be a scar he carried for life.

"Yeah, where you been, Johnny?" This whine came from the smaller man seated on the side of one of the beds.

Johnny glanced at Bobby, though it was Vince who held his attention.

"I was checking out the rez for our contact." Johnny's back was at the door. "Looks like he's not here yet."

Vince, his dirty T-shirt pulled tight over his bulging stomach, was leaning in close. "What do ya mean he's not here?"

It wasn't a complete lie. Johnny hadn't tried to make contact with the buyer yet, but he didn't feel like telling Vince and Bobby about what he had been doing for the past forty-eight hours.

"You're lying." He pushed Johnny up against the door.

Johnny gagged on Vince's foul breath and body odor.

"You trying to cut in on the action?" His fist held the front of Johnny's shirt and he was splattering Johnny's face with his anger.

Johnny felt disoriented and not just by the stink and violence radiating off of Vince. He was struck by his own ambivalence about the business deal he had set into motion four months ago. The deaths of his recently discovered son and his oldest friends left him disoriented.

"Relax, Vince, this deal is just going to take some time." Johnny hoped he sounded confident.

Vince jerked on Johnny's arm, forcing him into a chair at the small table.

Vince leaned over Johnny, his considerable bulk at Johnny's eye level. "I don't like the way this deal is going down, Larson."

Johnny pushed himself up and tried to move away from Vince. "Maybe I'll head back to Fort Thompson and take another look around?"

Vince reached for Johnny again. "You're not going anywhere without us."

Bobby wheezed from his perch. "That's right. We're sick of sitting here."

Vince shoved Johnny back toward the door. "Let's go."

Bobby popped up off the edge of bed and followed Vince and Johnny out the door.

Leaving Johnny's pickup parked at the motel, they rode in the car Vince and Bobby had driven up from Denver. Johnny sat shotgun while Bobby drove and Vince commanded the backseat, casually handling the handgun he kept with him while on business.

Bobby looked in the rearview mirror. "Where we goin, Vince?"

"Chamberlain. I need something to eat." Vince lifted his handgun to check on the safety. "Then Johnny here is going to find the contact and we are going to move those rifles and then get the hell outta here."

Susie's Oasis was an eating establishment well known in the area. Just off the interstate, it was a favorite of truckers and locals alike. Susie's served up a no-frills menu of local beef and homemade pies. The three men slid into a booth. Within minutes coffee was delivered and their orders were taken.

"I saw a pay phone at the front door. I'll try calling the Denver number I have."
Johnny worked with a pocketful of coins and dialed. He turned his back to the table where his partners waited. The call was picked up.

Johnny glanced over his shoulder at the booth, then moved back around and said. "I'm looking for Randall."

"This Johnny Larson?" The woman on the other end didn't wait for an answer. "Randall said to tell you to meet him at the cabin near the river tomorrow night. Bring the goods. Said he'll have the rest of the money for you."

The line went dead.

Johnny held on to the receiver a moment, resting his forehead against the front of phone box, then hung up and returned to the booth.

He slid onto the grimy, plastic seat and shrugged. "Sounds like he hasn't shown up yet."

Vince scowled, but was distracted with the arrival of their order. The waitress set their food in front of them, the Susie Special, chicken fried steak served on slices of white bread with mashed potatoes and smothered with brown gravy, and topped off their coffee.

They wolfed their meal, paid their bill and got back in the car.

Vince directed Bobby to a drive-through liquor. More beer and another bottle of whiskey.

Vince opened a can of beer, chugged for a minute, then let out a long burp. "Larson, I don't know what's going on with you. You take off for two nights and come back with your tail between your legs."

Johnny glanced around to Vince, who was seated again in the backseat. Vince was looking out the window, a beer can in one hand and in the other he held his gun.

Johnny turned back around, stared out the window for a few minutes then suggested. "I was thinking maybe we should move the rifles."

"What the hell's a matter with where they are?" Vince growled and opened another beer.

Thinking about the cache of hidden rifles hidden in his hometown's backyard, Johnny sighed deeply, puzzled over an unfamiliar feeling, regret.

"Nothing." He said. "Just thought we could get them down here closer to the reservation. I know a place that's been deserted for years."

Johnny directed Bobby to an abandoned ranch house and an old barn ten miles out of town. "This place is far off the road and close to Crow Creek."

"Uh-huh." Vince grunted an approval from the back seat.

Bobby got the car back on the main road to Kadota. They rode in silence for some time.

Johnny watched the open prairie roll by and chewed on his mustache. "Come to think of it, maybe there is an even better spot further west off the interstate."

"Enough with your pussfooting around," Vince snapped. "Don't know what the hell you're up to but it don't seem like you want this deal to go through."

"Yeah, what's the deal, Johnny?" Bobby grumbled as slowed down for the turn into the motel.

"Just trying to find a closer, safer spot is all." It was throwing him off balance trying to make nice with his partners. "I just want to make sure we don't get caught out with the guns and turned into the authorities."

"Seems to me you got cold feet, Larson." Vince was leaning forward from the back seat, his breath hot and beery on Johnny's neck. "There something you're not telling us?"

When the car came to a stop in front of their motel room, Johnny jumped out and headed for his pickup.

"Where you think you're going?" Vince was out of the backseat.

Johnny turned around. "Thought I'd take another look around town. See if I could get a little more information."

"You're not going anywhere." With his gun, Vince motioned Johnny to the door.

Bobby unlocked it and Vince pushed Johnny into the darkened room. A blast of foul hot air hit him as he stumbled through the piles of cast-off clothing strewn across the floor sprawling onto the floor.

Johnny caught his balance, heard the door close and the deadbolt slide shut. "What the hell?" He turned around in the dim light, trying to get his bearings.

"Shut up, Larson! I'm done with you." Vince pistol whipped him across the face. "I'm taking charge of this deal."

Johnny bent over, holding his eye. "God, Vince, what'd ya do that for?" Blood was seeping through his fingers.

Vince threw Bobby a rope. "Tie him up."

Wrists tied to the chair handles and his ankles bound together, Johnny moaned. He thought he might throw-up.

He could see a floating image of Vince across from him. His eye was swelling and his head was beginning to throb.

Bobby flipped on the TV and settled himself on the bed with a beer.

Vince pulled out a chair and the bottle of whiskey.

## Chapter 21

James found a spot among the vehicles haphazardly parked in the worn yard in front of Betty's house. He parked, turned off the motor, then waited by his truck until Howard came to push open the screen door and beckon him inside. James made his way to the front step, collecting his thoughts. He had no answers for the family about Thomas' death.

"James, thanks for coming." Howard's big shoulders were bent and his face was drawn, but his eyes under the heavy lids warmed at the sight of James.

James pulled off his hat as he entered the house. He could smell comfort food, beef stew, coffee and a spicy cinnamon cake.

"How's Betty doing?" James felt the sorrow in the house and let it sit in his heart for an instant, then mentally pushed some space into his thoughts. He was here as a friend but also as a law enforcement officer.

Howard led the way through the small front room to the back of the house.

"It's hard on her. Losing another of her kids."

Betty was sandwiched between two older women on a couch with sagging, worn cushions. James knew both women, Betty's sister Gladys and Evelyn Spotted Owl. Evelyn was a stalwart of the community. James had turned to her for advice more than once, as she often had a sense of what reservation issues were brewing below the surface. He wondered if he would need her counsel again in the coming days.

A little girl was pushed up next to Betty, resting on the old woman's knee and brushing her doll's hair.

Betty gave him a sad smile and motioned for him to pull up a chair.

"Thanks for coming by, James."

He'd spent only a few minutes with her yesterday when he'd come by to break the painful news. Today she looked worn and sorrowful. Her eyes behind her glasses were red rimmed.

"How ya doing, Betty?" He reached over to gently and briefly clasp her hand.

A younger woman came out from the kitchen and offered him a cup of coffee and a piece of cake. "Here ya go, James."

The coffee and cake gave him a minute to collect his thoughts. He knew that food and companionship were the two best ways to console. Betty's family and friends would have been with her since she first heard the news of Thomas. They would stay through the wake and funeral and would continue to check on her for the next days and weeks.

James set his empty coffee cup and plate on the floor and leaned over with his elbows on his knees.

Betty started talking. "Thomas had been so excited, ya know, about getting into the Community College down in Denver. Said he wanted to study welding."

James held Betty's eyes as she went on with remembering Thomas.

"He did so good in school. He even had some scholarships to go to that college in Denver." She was quiet for a moment then continued. "Thomas had ideas about how he would come back to the reservation and start a business."

She was quiet for a bit. She twisted a handkerchief in her hands while she talked about her nephew.

James reached over and placed his hand over her fretting fingers.

She began again. "He'd been happy with his job out at Franklin's."

She looked up at James and gave a weak smile. "He liked that he could give me some money. He liked to be helping out with what we needed."

A shadow crossed her face. "A few days ago there was a man who came around." She looked up at James, frightened. "He asked about where he could find Thomas."

"When was that, Betty, when he came to the house?" James asked quietly.

"It was on Saturday. I told him that Thomas worked out on a ranch and told him where it was." Her voice shook.

"Can you describe him?" Johnny's voice was gentle.

"A white man. Older." Betty stared at her twisting hands. "Don't know why I told him what he wanted to know."

"Do you remember what kind of car was he driving?" James asked.

"It was a old blue pickup." She looked up from her lap, her eyes full of tears.

Evelyn put her arm around her friend and looked up at

James. "You'll find out when we can pick up Thomas' body?"

James squeezed his lips together and nodded. He rested his hand on Betty's hands for a moment, then stood up, walked with his dishes to the kitchen and let himself out of the house.

James stepped outside, leaving Betty and her hurt. There was a low moaning sound as the branches of the trees crowding around the old house rubbed together in the wind. Dogs were barking nearby.

The day was starting to heat up. Horses were stomping off flies in the corral across the road. Heads down eating hay, their tails swished back and forth.

James backed his truck out of the yard and slowly headed through town toward the tribal police office on main street.

He was one of two officers who kept the peace on the adjoining reservations, Crow Creek and Lower Brule. They were responsible for investigations and arrests, and often settled disputes among families and neighbors. This week he was on his own as his partner was out of town visiting family in Minnesota.

The third person in their office was Janet, his partner's young cousin.

"Hey Janet." James came into the office. He walked to his desk and started looking through a stack of mail. "How's it going?"

Janet had recently graduated high school; she was working in their office for the summer before going to college in the fall. She answered phones, did paperwork, and kept the office running smoothly. She also served as reporter of tribal news, ranging from daily gossip to genuinely informative bits.

"Hi James." Her voice sounded odd. "It's good I guess."

James stopped what he was doing and looked at her. "What's going on?"

"It's nothing. Probably." She shot him a worried look. "It's just that, well, last night William came dragging in late."

James knew that Janet's brother, a couple years older than she, still lived at home with her and her parents.

Janet went on. "William has gotten caught up in this AIM business. The folks tell him to stay away from those people. They say AIM is just wanting to pick fights."

She continued, "I think AIM and their people should get the hell out of our business." Like many people on the two reservations, she resented the American Indian Movement's intrusion into the community.

"Anyway, he was acting all mysterious." She rolled her eyes. "Trying to keep a secret but dying to have me ask him about it.

"When I did ask him what he was talking about, he said, just wait -- in a couple days there will be action enough, here, to bring the crowds in from Pine Ridge and Rosebud." Janet frowned. "What's going on around here?"

He looked at her worried face. "I don't know, Janet, but I intend to find out."

James returned to his stack of mail though he was no longer focusing on the task. He needed to get out onto the reservations and find some concrete leads on the rumors that were flying around. He wanted to find out if it was true that Martha was on the reservation.

"James. Hey, James." He looked over at Janet. She had the phone in her hand. "Guess you didn't hear it ring. This is George Wilcox. He wants to talk with you."

Janet watched his face as James' expression reflected the conversation.

"What is it?" She asked when he hung up.

James picked up his hat and headed toward the door. "One of George's boys has been missing for nearly twenty-four hours."

"Oh gosh. His sons are pretty young. The oldest is maybe in seventh grade." Janet looked concerned.

"Looks like I'll be gone for awhile. Tracking down the rumors will have to wait." He headed out the door.

## Chapter 22

Vera stood with the fridge door open, looking for some lunch. Her quest was interrupted by a call from Lillian.

Lillian and her husband, Fred, lived just north of Ree Heights on a farm that had been in Lillian's family for two generations. Lillian raised chickens and quilted. She chaired the Women's Auxiliary and attended nearly all of the sporting events for her thirteen grandchildren.

Vera also knew Lillian watched her youngest grandson two mornings a week, likely accounting for her absence from the cafe earlier. Lillian didn't like missing out on the day's conversation. Fred, a patient good-humored husband, would have offered her the gist of the morning's news.

Lillian didn't waste time on niceties. "Vera, Fred just came in the house for his dinner and he was saying that you were asking about an old blue Ford pickup."

Vera could imagine Fred and the two hired men who worked for him seated in front of plates heaped with roast beef, mashed potatoes and gravy, along with helpings of Lillian's canned beans -- too early for garden beans. Sliced bread and butter would be on the table and, after the meal, a chocolate cake for their dessert.

Dinners on the farm were served at 12:00 sharp and involved a lot of calories. After the meal, the three men would stretch out on the couch or floor and close their eyes for twenty minutes. Restored, they would head back to the fields to work until near dark. In the late afternoon, Lillian would bring iced tea and cookies out to the fields. Finally, she'd serve them a light supper at about 8:30.

Lillian continued with her report. "Well, I was driving over to see Stella. Ya know, she isn't getting around too good with her broken wrist." Lillian's older sister, Stella, lived a few miles down the road beyond Lillian and Fred's place. Stella was as laid-back as Lillian was industrious. A retired teacher, Stella loved to read, grow flowers, and give her hand to writing poetry.

"She can't do any cooking with her wrist in a sling and I was taking her some supper -- I think it was Friday past. It was getting dark but I could see well enough and I'm sure it was a old blue Ford that passed me." When Lillian got started telling something, it was best to just stay quiet and not interrupt.

"One other thing, Vera," Lillian continued, "is that Stella -- she lives alone out on her place -- guess you know Don's been gone for a few years now -- well she'd been hearing noises out in one of their old sheds a few nights ago. She figured it was critters or bats bumping around."

"Thanks for your call, Lillian." Vera eased Lillian to the end of the conversation. "I'll pay Stella a visit this afternoon."


Stella, Mrs. Hughes to Vera, had been her teacher in her fifth and sixth grade years. The Ree Heights school was a hybrid of a country and a town school. Rural students rode the bus into town to go to school. The one-room schools were closed down to save money. Grades were combined in the four big rooms of the Ree Heights school, K- second together, third and fourth together, fifth and sixth together, and seventh and eighth together. High school students were similarly rounded up from Ree Heights and surrounding farms and ranches and bused to Miller to the county's only high school. Students from outlying ranches, forty-five miles out of town, often boarded in Miller during the school week.

Consolidation of the country schools had been unpopular at the time and had remained a bone of contention in the decade after the fact. Rural families felt they were losing some of their identity with the closing of their schools. Vera remembered the years her dad sat on the county school board. She knew her dad was more progressive than others in the community. She also knew he believed that, with fewer schools to support, the district could provide a more thorough curriculum to more students in a centralized location. Tempers ran hot in the community. He had come out to get in his car after one of those fiery school board meetings to find that a rock had been launched through his front window.

Stella was sitting out on her wide front porch when Vera pulled up in her yard. She set down her book and chortled. "Why, Vera Carlson, it's wonderful to see you!"

Vera remembered Mrs. Hughes's wide ranging interests, from paper mache to evolution. She credited Mrs. Hughes for kindling her first curiosities about the world beyond their small town.

She rose slowly from her rocker to give Vera a hug. "What brings you out here, dear?"

"Thought you could maybe help me with something, Stella." Vera smiled at Stella's curious expression.

With her good hand, Stella held on to Vera's elbow to steady herself and they went through the screen door into her kitchen.

"How're things going for you, Vera? I was so saddened by the death of your parents. How's Wally doing?" She seated Vera at her kitchen table and poured them both some coffee.

Talk ranged from an update on Wally to Stella's mending arm to how Vera was coping with the ranch. After looking at pictures of Stella's grandchildren, Vera got to the reason for her visit.

"Lillian mentioned that you'd heard some noises out in your shed the other night?" Vera wanted to take a look around but didn't want to worry her.

"Well that's true, Vera. With it being so warm at night lately, I've been sleeping with the windows open. I did hear some peculiar sounds out in the yards -- oh, maybe four or five nights ago."

"Is that right?" Vera noticed that Stella did not look particularly concerned. "Do you mind if I look around?"

"Go right ahead, dear. The shed is back behind the shop." Stella followed Vera out onto the porch and resettled in her rocker.

Mostly obscured from view by overgrown plum bushes, the shed was on the back of the property and accessible by a dirt trail that came off the main road. With its close proximity to the nearby field, Vera could guess the low-ceilinged wooden structure had been used for storing farm equipment at one time or another. Fresh tire tracks led to the building and she could see where the doors had recently been pulled open to the space inside. Cigarette butts littered the ground. Vera noticed parallel skid marks in the dirt floor that led out the door then stopped just beyond to where a truck likely was parked.

She walked back to the house and pulled up a matching rocker next to Stella. "It looks like someone might have been staying out there or maybe storing something out there but it is cleared out now."

Stella looked over at her. "Ya know, Vera, if someone needed a spot to rest, I don't mind. Seems like no harm was done."

Vera was quiet for a minute then asked, "Stella, did you ever know Johnny Larson?"

"Oh goodness, yes!" She chuckled. "That young man was full of life, but trouble! Don hired Johnny one summer to work for us."

She shook her head as she remembered.

"Johnny'd often show up late or not at all. Of course, he would have excuses but Don did not invite him back for another summer."

"Have you seen him again over the years?" Vera slid to the front of the rocker so she could face Stella more directly.

"No. Can't say that I have." She paused to think, then inquired, "Why do you ask?"

Then with a twinkle in her eye, Stella asked. "Are you investigating a case?"

Vera gave her a smile. "Well, Stella, I'm not quite ready to share my speculations just yet."

Vera pushed up from the rocker. "I really should get going. Thanks for the coffee." She leaned over and gave Stella a hug.

"Hope you will come back soon, dear, and fill me in on the details."

Driving slowly across the washboard lane from Stella's yard out to the main road, Vera dug through the glove box and found her sunglasses. A field of new oats shimmered blue-green in the afternoon heat while the heavy fragrance of blossoming plum trees scattered in the ditches wafted through the open windows.

She pursed her lips and frowned as she thought about Stella's unlocked door and open windows. In a small town nobody locks a door or takes their key out of their vehicles. It's part of the trusting environment that she had taken for granted growing up. Returning to Ree Heights she found the practice both endearing and unnerving. The safety of this community was now her responsibility.

Vera pushed open the front door of the Hand County Sheriff's Department office, a one-room affair, causing the the bell hanging over the door to ring.

"Hey there, Vera." Thelma's glasses balanced on her nose as she looked up over her typing. The smoke from her cigarette burning in the ashtray funneled upward in the breeze from the open door.

"Hi Thelma. How're you?" She saw only Thelma but asked. "Is Earl around?"

From what Vera could determine, Sheriff Earl Adams didn't leave his office unless it was entirely necessary. Thelma fielded phone calls that came in and managed whatever paperwork there was, while Earl drank coffee with whomever stopped by.

"He's in Pierre for a few days. Regional sheriffs conference -- said he'd be back on Wednesday and to make room in my freezer." Thelma gave a throaty laugh and then coughed a little.

Vera looked puzzled. "Your freezer?"

Thelma's eyebrows arched. "No doubt he's spending most of his time on a fishing boat with one of his buddies."

"Oh gotcha. What's he pulling out of the river?"

"Bass mostly. But he knows I prefer walleye."

Vera was beginning to adjust to the slow-paced tempo of law enforcement in a small town.

"How about Jerry? Is he around?" She hadn't had an opportunity yet to settle into the office or to get professionally acquainted with Jerry, the other deputy sheriff. She'd gone to high-school with his older brother and knew the family. She recalled Jerry as a cute, chubby little kid, maybe close to the same age as Wally.

"Jerry left a couple of hours ago to check out a barn fire near Wessington."

Vera walked back to the corner desk that she shared with Jerry and pulled open the drawers one by one. The desk was impressively neat. She took out a small tablet and a pen that she found in a mostly empty drawer.

She sat at the desk and wrote out the timeline and details of the events for the past two days, wondering if there were connections she hadn't spotted.

Thelma turned in her chair and waited for Vera to finish.

Taking a long drag from the last of her cigarette, she crushed it out and asked. "Finding anything to go on with that kid's death?"

"Waiting on the autopsy report from Albert."

"What about the tribal police?" she queried. "Are they providing support?"

"Yeah, they are. Well, he is. James Broken Hand's in charge of the investigation from the Crow Creek end of things."

"Is that right?" Another arched eyebrow.

Miller is larger than Ree Heights, but still a small town. Thelma seemed to be skimming through her catalogued history of the area and the activities of the people in it.

Vera waited a beat, then changed the subject. "I'm headed over to talk with Albert now. See what he's learned."

She rose and headed for the door before there could be more questions. "See ya later, Thelma."

In her youth, Vera had never had an occasion to visit the small brick building that sat behind the old stone courthouse, but she had always been curious.

She walked into the dark waiting room that fronted Albert's coroner's lab. Sunlight filtered through the drawn venetian blinds. The door jangled closed behind her.

"Hello?"

In the time it took for her eyes to adjust to the dim interior, Albert came through a door wearing a lab coat. "Hello Vera."

"Hi Albert. How're you? Thought I'd stop by." Vera filled in both sides of their conversation. "You mentioned on the phone that you have an idea about how Thomas died?"

He turned, pushed open a door leading to the lab. "Follow me, please."

She was hit by a whush of icy air.

"Interesting case." Albert offered over his shoulder as he led her to a shrouded body lying on a steel table in the middle of the room.

They moved to stand next to the body. The tang of disinfectant assaulted Vera's nose while her attention was drawn to the drain in the cement floor. It appeared damp from a recent rinse.

"No obvious marks on the body," Albert reported as he pulled back the sheet covering the top part of the body.

Even in death, Thomas' body seemed youthful and strong. She noticed a detail she had missed before, a dimpled chin.

"As I said, an interesting case." Albert moved around to the opposite side of the table. "It would appear he suffered a heart event."

"You mean he had a heart attack?" she asked.

"An intriguing case." Albert seemed genuinely engaged in the conversation -- animated even. "I have made a surprising discovery."

Albert pushed up his glasses and glanced at her. "His heart just stopped pumping."

Vera looked at Albert then down at the body and asked again, "But it wasn't a heart attack?"

"Following a suspicion I had, I thoroughly examined the contents of the stomach." Albert turned to a small covered bowl placed nearby. "There I found the remains of chocolate and cashews."

Addressing the body before him, Albert continued, "Clearly this young man was allergic to tree nuts, and in particular, to cashews."

Not understanding, Vera grunted a "Huh?"

"It appears that the deceased ate a candy bar with cashews and had a severe reaction. The nuts caused an anaphylaxis reaction."

Albert explained, "In some cases the symptoms of anaphylaxis can bring on dangerously low blood pressure which can result in a loss of consciousness and in extreme cases, death."

"You're saying Thomas had died from eating candy?"

"It's most likely the young man had never been exposed to cashews before and yes, tragically, died from that first experience of eating them."

"That's terrible. How often does that happen?" Vera suddenly felt exposed to dangers she had never heard of before.

"Some people think it requires repeated exposure to the anaphylactic trigger, in fact, a first experience can sometimes be fatal."

She thought of the candy wrapper they had found in Thomas' pocket.

Vera stepped out of the dark lab into the late afternoon sunshine and blinked hard.

"Heard you'd move back."

She whirled around and found herself face to face with Mac MacDonald. Tall with a beefy build and a buzz cut, Mac was good looking and he knew it.

Had always known it.

"Oh, hi Mac." She'd known Mac in high school.

Actually in a graduating class of fifty-five students, she'd known everyone in high school. A big fish in a small pond, Mac had basked in the glory of a successful high school sports career.

"Looks like city life agreed with you, Vera." Mac's intense blue-eyed stare unhinged her. Always had. And not in an especially good way.

"Oh yeah. Guess it has." She looked at him, tried a slight smile. "How're you?"

"Guess you heard I took over running the elevators and auction from Dad?" He watched her closely to make sure she looked impressed. "Business should pick up again as soon's this drought breaks."

"Nice." She nodded, playing her part in the conversation.

"You been gone a long time, Vera. Think you can handle small town living?" He'd backed her up against her vehicle.

"Not sure of my plans just yet." She glanced around. No one else around. She'd parked behind the courthouse.

151

"Maybe I'll see more of you if you're staying in the area." His breath was minty, overlaying his apparent smoking habit.

"Maybe. Well, I'd better get going."

She turned, opened the car door and got in. He stepped aside as she drove away. In her rearview mirror she watched as Mac continued to stare at her.

She wiped her palms on her jeans.


When Vera pulled up in front of Wally's garage, the tall bay doors were closed. She quickly went to the side door and let herself in.

"Wally? Ya here?" She called to him as she moved through the living quarters out into the shop. "Everything OK? Ya closed up shop little early today?"

"You're a good girl. Take it easy." She could hear her brother talking to someone.

She followed his voice to the back of the shop.

Vera found Wally on a rug, spread on the concrete floor, with a small mound of black fur on his lap. The puppy was licking his face and wagging a stubby tail.

"Oh wow! She's so cute!" She sat down beside her brother and reached over to pet the wiggling puppy.

She let it chew on her fingers and asked. "Where'd she come from?"

Wally watched the puppy as he answered. "The folks across the street brought her over this morning. Said their dog had a litter a few weeks ago. Wondered if I wanted a puppy."

"Dang. She's cute." With a little growl, the pup tugged on her shoelaces.

"Yeah she is." He picked her up and set her back in his lap. "I need to figure out a bed for her."

Vera stood up. "Guess I should get going."

Wally didn't look up. "Sure. See ya later."

Vera closed the shop door behind her. She looked across the street and waved at the older woman watering a bed of flowers. She breathed in deeply and smiled.

## *Chapter 23*

It was late in the afternoon when Randall and Martha crossed the bridge over the Missouri then turned off the road onto to a muddy trail. He had gotten to Pine Ridge earlier that morning and had spent the day talking over plans with the others. Martha had come along with him to Crow Creek; she had business on the reservation.

They found the old cabin, set up on the bank from the shoreline to protect it from spring flooding. Randall saw a pickup pulled up on the far side of the building and parked behind it.

Two young men stumbled out the door, shading their eyes.

"Hi Randall. Martha." William swaggered in front of the visitors. "We're ready for you."

Randall looked around then asked, "Where are the others? Thought you said you had people on this sorry reservation who wanted to be involved in making some changes?"

"Don't worry." William bluffed. "There'll be more once they see we've got the muscle."

"Oh yeah?" Randall shook his head and sighed.

"We got a place for the rifles." William spoke up again. "Follow me."

Squelching through the mud to where the ground began to slope up, William led the others a short distance from the cabin, then pointed to a door framed further up in the hillside. "We can hide them in that dugout. It's big enough and it's dry. I've checked."

Randall grunted his approval.

The four of them turned around to face out toward the river.

"Hey, cousin, how's it feel to be back on the rez?" Leonard directed his comment to Martha. He was a little in awe of his older cousin. She was beautiful and aloof. Though the dusk was falling quickly under the overhanging bluffs, she still wore the dark sunglasses that hid her eyes.

"It stinks here just the way I remember it." She wiped her boots on the grass, boots ingrained with swirls of red and gold.

"I'm not planning on staying." She faced the river as she spoke. "Only here long enough to find my son and get him off the rez."

"Good luck with that." Leonard knew a few things about this town that his cousin had maybe forgotten. "James isn't going to let you near him."

"We'll see about that." Her mouth pressed into a straight line as she stared out across the water.

William looked at Randall and said, "There's a white guy in town says he's looking for you."

Randall glanced at him. "You talked to him?"

"No, just heard that he's been asking around." William pulled off his hat and wiped his forehead. "Heard he's a big guy. Bald. Driving a Lincoln with Colorado plates."

Randall scowled. "The Colorado plates sound right but that description doesn't sound like Larson."

Randall headed back down the hill to the cabin with others following.

William wanted some action. "What are we going to do now?"

Mostly talking to himself, Randall said. "Sounds like the weapons are in the area. I got the money from AIM. Just got to find this guy and finish the deal."

He turned abruptly and faced them. "There'll be others coming in from Pine Ridge and Rosebud later tonight."


## Chapter 24

Driving south toward Crow Creek, with the long horizontal stretch of the sun moving toward the western skyline, Vera felt her shoulders and neck begin to relax. Though she hadn't lived in the area in over a decade, she remembered the slow progression of summer evenings out on the prairie. How the light fades ever so gradually. How dusk offers a gentler, friendlier warmth when the heat of day gives way to cooler temperatures. How the winds calm in the evening. And how, stretched out along the rim of the horizon, the sunset is a display of color and cloud-play. Full darkness is delayed until well past ten o'clock.

She wanted to talk with James, to talk through the jumble of information she had collected. Fort Thompson was due south of Ree Heights about thirty-five miles.

She slowed down at a turn in the road and let herself have a long look at the deserted buildings set back from the road. She and James used to meet at this halfway point between their two houses.

She felt guilty about the way she had left him all those years ago, without saying good-bye or telling him about the real reasons for her decision. No surprise there would be awkwardness in reconnecting with him now.

Vera drove through town and parked in front of the Crow Creek - Lower Brule tribal office. Since it was early evening, she had wondered if anybody would still be there. She pushed open the front door.

"Oh hi! Can I help you?" A young woman sitting behind a desk set down her a magazine and brightened. On the desk were a bottle of nail polish, an apple core, and a diet Coke.

"I'm Vera Carlson from the Hand County Sheriff Department. I'm working with James Broken Hand investigating the death of Thomas Yellow-Knife."

The young woman's face crumpled. "Thomas was such a good guy."

"I'm sorry. Guess you knew Thomas?" Vera responded gently.

"Yes, I've known him all my life." The young woman wiped the corners of her eyes. "He just graduated. Seemed like he had

plans, like he was going somewhere. Like he'd be something."
Her voice trailed off.

Vera thought again about the differences between law
enforcement in a small town where everyone knew each other
and law enforcement in a city.

Remembering some protocol, the young woman added.
"I'm Janet by the way. It's nice to meet you."

Vera gave her a brief smile. "I am looking for James. Is he
around?"

"He stopped by earlier this afternoon but he hasn't come
back to the office. I was waiting for him but was about to give up
and close the office." Janet explained and then added, "I doubt
he'll come back here, guessing he'll go straight home instead."

She glanced at Vera and asked. "You know how to get
there?"

Janet's directions led Vera to a small house on the
outskirts of town. In the last of the evening light, Vera parked,
then walked through the lilac bushes lining the walkway up to the

house. Trumpet vines grew up on one side of his front door. A towering cottonwood tree dominated the yard.

She didn't see James' truck, and with no answer to a knock on the door, she settled herself on the top step to wait. Cars, trucks and toy army men covered the steps and along the walk.

She leaned back against the porch railing, closed her eyes, and listened to the sounds of nightfall, frogs croaking in the creek nearby and mourning doves settling in the trees around the house. Eventually she heard a vehicle on the road.

James parked near the barn and walked her way in the growing dusk.

"Hi. How's it going?" Vera spoke to him through the dusk.

James was moving slowly. He shook his head. "God. It's been a rough afternoon."

She paused then asked. "Ya want to talk about it?"

"Maybe later." James stopped in front of her. "You called last night. Sorry I hadn't gotten you called back."

She stood up. "It's Ok. I enjoyed the drive down here. Thought I could fill you in what I've learned."

He gave her a slight nod and walked past her up the steps to the front door.

"Come on in." He held the door open for her, let the meowing cat into the house, then led the way through the small house, turning on lights as he went along.

She noticed children's books stacked on the coffee table and wooden blocks piled in the corner.

James leaned over to scratch the cat. "Are you hungry?"

She followed him as he continued through the house into the kitchen, pulled on the string for the overhead light above the sink.

He pulled out a chair for her at the small rectangular kitchen table and asked, "How about you, Vera? Are you hungry? Do you need to get back or can you stay for some supper?"

She fumbled a little. "I don't want to interrupt your routine, but yeah, sure, some supper would be good."

He opened the refrigerator door, light outlined his bent figure. The cat curled around his legs. She looked away from him quickly as he stood up from his search.

"Hope you like chili?" He pulled out a container with their supper and a beer for each of them.

Vera watched him as he worked -- filling the cat bowl in the corner, emptying the chili into a saucepan, bringing out bowls and silverware.

"I saw Albert a couple of hours ago. He wanted to let Thomas' family know that they could pick up the body tomorrow morning."

James stopped and turned to her. "I should call his aunt and uncle now, so they can make plans for his wake and funeral."

Vera could hear his voice, low and soothing, talking on the phone in the next room.

She came around the corner and asked soundlessly. "Bathroom?"

He pointed down the hall.

She flipped on the bathroom light. A fishnet bag of toy boats hung from the tub faucet handle. Hair products and makeup covered the top of the small cabinet in the corner.

When she returned to the kitchen, James was at the stove.

He looked over at her. "Sounds like they'll have Thomas' funeral on Wednesday morning. I'll go tomorrow morning to pick up the body."

Alternately stirring the warming chili on the stove and leaning against the counter, James sipped a beer and listened to her. She started with her visit to the coroner.

As she talked, he brought out a loaf of homemade bread and a cutting board.

When he heard Vera give Albert's account of how Thomas died, he lowered the bread knife to look at her. "You're saying a nut allergy killed Thomas? That's terrible."

James dipped out chili into their bowls then turned off the light above the sink. A small lamp on the table lit a circle around them.

"This is delicious." She hadn't realized she was so hungry. "Thanks, James, for feeding me."

Finished, feeling full and relaxed, Vera leaned back in her chair, sipped on the last of the beer, and continued with details of the past two days. She told him about Johnny's early morning visit and taking gas. She explained Johnny's connection to her parents, and also gave a brief description of the last time she had seen him, arriving in his bush plane the summer she was eleven.

James stood to clear the dishes, turning from the sink, he asked. "Any guesses why he's in the area?"

Vera glanced at James, then back to the empty bottle in her hands. Controlling a tremor in her voice, she said. "Yesterday afternoon someone walked into Wally's shop and stole his rifle."

She looked up at him directly. "I think it was Johnny who stole it."

"Wait. Why do think it was Johnny?"

"Wally only saw the back of the man's head, but he could describe the vehicle. An old blue Ford. Johnny's pickup."

Vera had gone quiet. James sat across from her again, waiting for her to continue. She reached into her back pocket.

"I think Johnny was spending time with Thomas. I found this up at the old Cedar Grange where I think Johnny was hiding out." James leaned over a school photo of a young boy that Vera laid on the table.

James gave a low whistle. "That's Thomas. Maybe at about ten years old?"

"Thomas' aunt Betty told me an older white man had come by Friday afternoon asking about Thomas. He was driving a blue pickup." He glanced at her for confirmation. "That's Johnny's, isn't it?"

Vera set two coins on the table. "These are Algerian dinar. One is from Thomas' pocket and the other is one Johnny gave me on that visit twenty years ago."

James moved to put the tea kettle on. "What kind of business was he in?"

"He flew munitions into warring countries the U.S. wanted to support but didn't want recognition for. He traveled all over the world delivering weapons. Apparently he's out of that business now and living in Denver."

"Or maybe not? Word on the reservation is someone is moving weapons in. Financed by AIM." James abruptly moved to pull off the whistling tea kettle.

Vera came to stand by James. She looked up at him. "I had coffee this morning down at the Cafe and described Johnny's truck. The small town grapevine works so well, by noon I got a call about a spotting made Friday night of a pickup of that description. Seems it was loaded with crates. I was also told about a shed in that same area that seemed to have been visited recently in the night. I checked it out and it looks like crates had been stored there recently."

She faced him as the steam from the tea heated the space between them.

James digested the information. "You think those crates could be filled with weapons?"

She nodded slowly.

He continued, looking at her intently. "And those weapons are intended for someone on the reservation?"

He let out a long breath. "I need to find out who here wants to buy them."

They moved back to the table with their mugs of tea. James set out sugar and spoons. The front and back doors were opened, the screen doors allowed a cooling breeze through the house. The sound of cicadas and crickets from the yard helped to fill the lull in the conversation.

"James, what happened today?" Vera wanted more conversation with him.

James let out a long sigh and stared into a corner of the kitchen.

"I got called out to the Wilcox ranch this afternoon." He rubbed his eyes with the  heels of both hands, sighed deeply, then took a sip of the hot tea. "One of their boys -- their twelve-year-old -- had been missing for more than a day. They'd checked with neighbors and nobody'd seen him."

Vera leaned forward, eyebrows furrowed, listening.

James stared at his hands around the tea cup and shook his head slowly. "We drained the oats bin and found his body."

"Oh my god. He'd jumped in the bin." Vera teared up. "That's something my cousins and I used to do. My dad would get so mad."

James sighed again. "What kid doesn't love to jump into the cool slippery oats?"

"I'm so sorry, James," Vera said quietly.

They sat together then, silently, for a minute.

Vera drank the last of her tea, noticed the darkness and roused herself.

She stood up. "Thanks for supper."

He looked up at her from his spot at the table. "You haven't asked me yet." His mouth pulled up on one side to half smile. "I know your skills of observation."

Vera tilted her head to one side, returned the half smile, and waited.

"I have a son. His name is Lucas. He turns six next week. He's out on the ranch with my folks this week."

Vera looked at him and smiled. "That's wonderful, James."

She sat back down."I know you are a great dad."

He continued. "My wife, Martha, moved out a year ago. Life in this small town and being tied down with a family didn't suit her."

She nodded her head slightly. Vera wondered if her face was betraying her own recurring guilt. She, too, had left James. She, too, couldn't handle the idea of living in a small town.

He finished answering the last of Vera's unspoken questions. "My sister, Sandra, lives with Lucas and me. She's a nurse in Chamberlain and works the night shift three times in a week. She stays over those nights and lives here the rest of the week. She's a big help with Lucas."

"Oh, I see, yeah, that's good." Vera felt her shoulders relax then got to her feet again.

He walked her to the door. "Are you missing the city, Vera? And your life back there?"

"I do miss it." She looked up at him. "Truthfully, I would never have moved back to the area except for Wally. He needs me around."

"Right. You do what you have to do when your family needs you." James pushed open the screen door and followed her out onto the small front porch.

"I am starting to adjust to living under the community microscope again." Vera looked up at him again and gave him a small smile. The stars were bright over his head and shoulders. "It's getting easier."

The moon shone across the prairie as she drove back home.

James' last comment kept repeating in her mind. "You know, I never left. Not for long anyway. When I came back from college I found that I was needed -- by my family and by the tribe. There are times when it feels pretty claustrophobic for sure. But more of the time I appreciate the feeling of belonging and of feeling necessary."

## Chapter 25 -- Tuesday morning

Pulled from a deep sleep, Vera was instantly annoyed. Dogs were barking.

She pushed herself out of bed and squinted down from her bedroom window. In the early morning light she could see that Johnny's old pickup was again in the yard. She stood for a minute at the window but she didn't see him.

She found jeans and a sweatshirt in a pile on the floor, slipped on tennis shoes, and ran downstairs. She called the dogs into the house then went out to look around the parked truck. She opened the door of the truck and was leaning in to dig through the glove box when she heard a now familiar voice behind her.

"Sorry about dragging you into this, Vera."

She swung around. Dried blood crusted Johnny's nose, lip and chin. Both eyes were swollen, the right eye was completely shut. He pulled his head up and squinted his left eye at her before his head sagged forward again. He was bent over holding his side.

"What's going on, Johnny?" She stepped toward him but stopped short when two men moved up next to him.

"Who the hell are you?" Vera was backing up. "What do you want?"

The bigger one pointed a handgun at her. "Get in the truck."

She took her eyes off the gun to glance at Johnny. "What did you do to him?"

He moved toward her and grabbed her arm, pulling her toward the truck. "Get in. You're driving."

He pushed her behind the wheel of the old blue pickup then got in the passenger side. She could hear the dogs going crazy in the house.

The other one, his arms covered with the tattoos, disappeared behind the barn then drove out in a dented and rusted Lincoln. He got out and pushed Johnny into the backseat. She could see that Johnny put up no resistance.

With his gun resting across his lap, the Big One directed her to take the gravel road heading east. The car, carrying Johnny and Tattoos, was close behind in the cloud of dust blown up from the road.

"Where are we going?" she asked.

He growled at her. "Just drive."

Out of the corner of her eye, she looked over at her passenger. The last buttons on his shirt didn't close, his belly rolled over the top of his pants. He held the handgun casually on his thigh, used it to direct her to turn the truck onto a lesser section line road that wound its way up into the hills.

Another quick glance confirmed what she thought she had noticed. On the knuckles of his hand were the markings of a prominent gang. She had seen markings like those while working the streets of Minneapolis.

"What you looking at? Keep your eyes on the road."

"Johnny show you around here?" Johnny knew these hills from his youth. Her concern for his injuries flipped to anger and disgust.

She glanced in the rearview mirror to see the old car straddling the deep ruts, its undercarriage brushing the tall grass that grew in the middle of the little-used road. They were heading toward the top of the hills that overlooked Ree Heights and a summer pasture where Leona ran a small herd of cattle.

Vera stopped the truck in front of a gate in the barbwire fence.

Her passenger waved his gun toward the gate. "Open it." His elbow rested in the open window.

She took her time with it, pulling the gate post toward herself. She slid the top guide loop of baling wire off the post, then lifted the post out of the bottom loop. She pulled the gate open across the new grass, laying it down away from the tracks that led through the pasture. She made her way slowly back to the truck.

She climbed back in and put the truck in gear. "You guys aren't from around here."

"You got that right," the Big One snarled. "Not planning on staying long,"

"How do you know Johnny? Last I heard he was in Denver. Is that where you're from?"

Getting no reply, she continued, "I'm just wondering cause you guys stick out like sore thumbs. Chances are people have already noticed you and that boat of a car you're driving."

She added, "Seriously, it's hard to hide around here."

"Don't worry about us, Sugar. Johnny's been showing us around after dark. We been here longer than you think."

He looked at her and scowled. "Johnny some kind of relative of yours?"

"He was a friend of my parents." Vera glanced at him. "Lived here a long time ago."

The pickup bumped slowly across the pasture.

She asked, "Looks like that you and Johnny had some kind of disagreement?"

"Nothing you need to know about."

Vera could see Leona's black Angus cattle in the near distance -- their heads were down -- grazing their way in a westerly direction away from the vehicles. The new calves were staying close to their mothers. She wondered if Leona would be out this way today checking cows.

"OK. Far enough." He had her stop near to an old homestead. The Lincoln pulled up next to the pickup. He motioned her out of the pickup while Tattoos dragged Johnny from the backseat of the car.

Still visible poking through the ground, Vera could see the foundation stones of a long-abandoned home. She knew the sod walls and roof would have long since crumbled and rejoined the prairie. Bent and weathered lilac bushes grew up alongside the old foundation. Nearby Vera saw a healthy rhubarb plant with its green to red stalks spreading wide leaves. Over the cooling motors pinging softly, Vera could hear meadowlarks singing in the tall grass.

Debris from a life long gone was scattered across the area, rotted boards and baling wire, a small rusted-out cook stove with its bent pipe poking out of the grass along with a broken-handled plow partially buried in the earth. The Homestead Act of 1868 encouraged many eager, but often unprepared, "farmers" and their families to come west and settle out on the prairie. Harsh living conditions allowed only the most hardy to survive.

Vera's attention was drawn to a cellar within the foundation. She knew a root cellar would have been used by the family to store potatoes, carrots, beets and onions grown in their garden as well as the salted beef and other provisions needed for the family's survival through the winter months. She also knew the cellar would have provided the only protection against the tornadoes that skip across the plains in the summer months.

The grass around the cellar was flattened. Someone had been there not too long ago. The cellar was about six x six foot and a little over five feet deep; Vera knew the walls were lined with rocks while the floor would be dirt. The early morning sun cast a shadow across the cellar's opening. Looking more closely down into the depths, she could see that the cellar was again in use.

Vera wondered how Johnny and these city thugs could have moved crates into and out of Stella's shed, transported them up here and unloaded them without detection? Vera shook her head. The level of local surveyance into other people's business had obviously slipped of late.

"So Johnny," Vera looked at a bent-over Johnny standing next to her, directing her questions to him. "Looks like you're still in the gun-running business?"

He looked up at her and grunted something she couldn't understand.

"You led strangers into my town and hid weapons on my Aunt Leona's land." She aimed her comments to a balding spot she could see on top of his head surrounded by a fringe of reddish gray curly hair. "If you weren't hurt already, I'd hurt you myself."

"Enough." The Big One waved the gun from Vera to Johnny. "Johnny got himself into this mess."

"Why am I in this mess?" Vera's voice raised with her level of frustration.

"As you can see, Johnny's not fit to work this morning."

Vera glanced at Johnny, bent over holding his left arm with his right hand.

The Big One continued. "You'll do fine."

Pointing with the handgun from her to the cellar, "Get down there. You're going to unload those crates. "

Together Vera and Tattoos heaved and swung crates up out of the cellar. There were eight crates total, each filled with what Vera figured was maybe a dozen rifles. Nearly a hundred rifles -- and if she and James were right -- to be delivered to South Dakota reservations.

Finished with the task, Vera crawled out of the cellar. The early morning sun had warmed things up and she was dripping sweat. Tattoos looked wilted as well. Johnny was sitting in the grass, head down.

"Load them into the truck." The Big One again gestured to Vera with his gun. He looked over at his partner. "You help her."

"Geez, Vince, why I gotta do all the work?" Tattoos wheezed his complaints. "I need a rest. And a cigarette."

"You'll get a rest when you're done. Now get back to work."

Vera's arms were shaky from fatigue by the time she and Tattoos finished swinging the crates onto the bed of the pickup.

She leaned over, resting her hands on her thighs, catching her breath.

Standing upright again, she noticed that Vince, she now knew his name, was distracted with supervising Tattoos in tying down the crates.

She bolted for the car door, pulled it open and reached to turn the key in the ignition. She glanced in the direction of Vince then dropped on the seat just as a bullet shattered the window beside her covering her with glass.

"All right. All right. Stop firing!" Vera yelled from inside the car. She slowly sat up and with her hands in the air, slid her way over the glass and out of the car.

Vince grabbed her arm and backhanded her. She fell to the ground. He leaned over, pulled her up and pushed her toward Johnny. "Get him in the cellar."

She went over to Johnny, put her arm under his elbow and tried to pull him to a stand. He moaned and dropped to the ground.

Vince ordered Tattoos. "Git over there and help her."

Tattoos took Johnny's other elbow and jerked him to his feet. Together they dragged him toward the cellar.

Johnny was bleeding again. With a closer look, Vera could see that Johnny had been shot. His skin was pasty and slick and his breathing shallow.

As Vera stood next to Johnny trying to figure out a gentle way of lowering him down, she heard movement behind her. A hard shove pushed Johnny forward.


Some time later Vera awoke to a powerful headache and considerable disorientation. Darkness. A smell of earth. Her head throbbed. Her right cheek was tender to the touch. She gingerly probed a deep wet cut on the back of her scalp. Reaching out and down, she could feel the rocky walls and dirt floor and then remembered where she was.

She heard a moan and some breathing nearby and the events of the morning flooded in. Her head pounding, she crawled toward the sound. Johnny wasn't dead, at least. She could smell blood and body odor coming off of him. She pulled him to a narrow band of sunlight filtering through the cracks in the ceiling.

The gunshot to his side was the most serious, though she figured if he hadn't died from it yet, it might not be life-threatening if she could get them out of there and get him to a doctor.

"Johnny, hey, you're going to be OK. You just need to hang in there." She tore off and used the sleeves of her sweatshirt to bandage the wound.

No response from Johnny.

There wasn't room enough to stand straight so Vera crouched and crawled along feeling the covering over the cellar. It seemed to be an old door of some kind, possibly weighed down with large rocks. It wasn't budging when she pushed up. Exhausted from the effort, she laid back down to rest.

## Chapter 26

James couldn't sleep. Hadn't slept much all night. Couldn't turn off his brain. Were the rumors he had dismissed true? Were there guns on the reservations? Were there outsiders on the reservation who wanted to blow his community apart? Was Martha among them? He needed to warn his parents.

With first light, he got up and started coffee then walked out to the barn. His mare nuzzled him for attention while he watered her then let her out in the small padlock. He watched her for a minute as she trotted out into the tall grass still wet from the early morning dew. She shook her head then bent to graze. Her coat of deep red was dappled in shadow as the sun broke through the trees.

James walked back into the house and stopped at the phone in the hallway. He wanted to talk with Lucas, check in with his folks. He let the phone ring and ring, finally setting down the receiver. His forehead furrowed.

He dialed Vera's number and waited. No answer.

James backed his pickup under the shade of an old cottonwood. Their broad leaves clicked and clacked in the wind. In the bed of the truck rested a plain pinewood box. Thomas' body would rest in Betty's house during the hours of the wake, which would last through the day and night until his burial the next morning. Men came out of the house to help James carry the coffin into the living room.

Sawhorses had been set up in the middle of the room, ready to serve as a platform for the coffin. Folding chairs were stacked against the walls, ready to be unfolded around the coffin.

Some women were in the kitchen making coffee while others were setting out food on card tables. A group of men were in the corner making their drum circle, talking in hushed voices.

The Elders, both women and men, were seated on the couch and easy chairs which had been pushed back against the walls. They would move forward soon, around the coffin, to lead prayers to guide Thomas' spirit into the next world. They would watch over Thomas and support him in his journey. Following tradition and through experience, the community knew how to come together to honor the dead.

James paused in the doorway, hat in hand, taking in the scene. Though he planned to come back to sit with Betty and Howard, just now he needed to get out on the reservation to hunt down the people and weapons that threatened the peace and harmony of his community.

## Chapter 27

Some time later, Vera awoke again. She noticed the sunlight was coming in more vertically than earlier and realized it must be mid-day. She could see Johnny's prone body. She moved over to check on him.

"You're alive." She let out a long breath. "Stay unconscious. It's a good plan."

She moved to sit with her back against the cool earthen wall. She closed her eyes listening to the wind and remembering.

She and her cousins would come to this pasture and the Pretty Draw, as they called it, on Sunday afternoons in the summer months with Leona and Henry. The Pretty Draw seemed magical. It was deep draw cut into the hillside by a small creek that ran for only a few weeks in early summer. Thick with willows and chokecherry bushes along with grasses not found up on top of the hills, the narrow ravine dropped steeply into the pasture below where it spread out again and disappeared back into the rolling prairie.

Sitting in the cool shade of cottonwoods lining the creek, her aunt would tell them stories about Ree Indians. One of the stories that captured her imagination was about how the tribe had driven bison over the cliff. Leona would look up and point out where the bison would have plunged over the edge above them. She explained how the hunters would cloak themselves with the skins of bison. They would crouch down and move along with the herd until the bison were in a position near to the cliff. Then the hunters would rise up, throw off the hides and scare the stampeding bison over the drop-off. Because the bison didn't necessarily die in the fall, more hunters waited below to kill those bison that had been badly wounded. Women waited there to begin the butchering process. Vera could picture it all. Bison thundering their way toward and over the cliff, their hoofs shaking the ground, and their screams as they hit the ground below. Leona made sure her audience understood the incredible bravery and resourcefulness of the tribe.

Vera was pulled back to the present when she heard the sound of a motor in the distance. It was coming closer.

The motor quieted and a door closed.

"Vera!" She could hear Leona. "Vera!"

"Down here." Vera called through the slats in the ceiling. "In the cellar."

In short order Leona was standing over her. "Vera, are you OK? What the hell is going on?"

"I'm OK but Johnny is down here with me and he's hurt."

"It's going to take a few minutes to get you out of there."
Vera heard her move off and then heard the sound of her vehicle
again.

"Leona's here. She's going to get us out." She said to her
unconscious companion. "I'm not sure what she has in mind."

There was no response from Johnny.

Vera could see her aunt through the crack at edge of the
covering. She watched Leona back up her pickup to the cellar.
She took out a rope from the toolbox of her truck. She tied one
end of the rope to the hitch of her truck and the other end around
a rock that rested on top of the door covering the cellar. Leona
got back in her truck, put it into a low gear and pulled the rock off
the covering.

Leona reversed a few feet, untied the rock, then walked
back to the cellar to repeat the process.

Vera sat down to wait. "Damn it all to hell." She could hear
Leona muttering as she worked.

Vera heard Leona's truck grind into first gear and a second rock was pulled off.

Leeona was back, talking to herself as she worked. "What the hell is going on around here?" Vera heard another rock get rolled off.

"Damn it. Did Johnny bring this on?" Vera heard Leona through the cracks above her as she tied the end of rope to the door covering.

"Lord have mercy, I am too old to have this much anxiety." Vera heard her aunt, then heard the slam of the truck door and the gunning of the motor.

The covering over the cellar slid off.

Vera turned to Johnny. The bright light revealed the sweatshirt bandage soaked through with blood. The dull red contrasted with the pallor of his skin. His breathing was barely audible.

Leona knelt down to look down into the dark cellar.

Seeing Johnny, she let out a loud gasp. "Oh my god!"

Her face registered relief and concern when she saw her niece.

Vera guessed that her face had bruised and there was blood in her hair.

"Am I glad to see you, Leona." Vera looked up at her aunt, her corkscrew-permed hair haloed by the intense sunlight overhead.

"Humph." Leona seemed to be taking in the situation.

Vera looked from Leona to Johnny and back up to where Leona had just been standing. "How are we going to get him out of here?"

She had disappeared from sight.

A few minutes later, Vera saw the door covering again. "Vera, I'm going to lower this door down to you. I want you to hoist Johnny onto it, best as ya can."

Vera guided the door as Leona slid it down into the cellar, keeping the top of it at the lip of the cellar opening. Vera tugged and pulled Johnny's nearly inert body up onto the door.

"OK, that's good," Leona coached.

"Now, I'm going to pull him up outta there." Vera heard the motor start up again. The door with Johnny on it began to slide up and out of the cellar. Vera grasped at his body to keep it from sliding off the platform.

Vera climbed the rock steps now visible in the daylight.

Leona handed Vera a handkerchief and a baseball cap from the cab of her truck. "Here, tie this around your head, you're bleeding."

"Thanks, Leona." Vera offered her a teary half smile.

"You gave me a fright, gal." She gave Vera a quick hug. "Now let's get you two to the hospital."

Leona had moved her truck closer to Johnny. He moaned as they dragged him through the tall grass and laid him up onto the bench seat in the truck.

Leona got into the driver's seat, Johnny's head resting on her lap.

"Ya sure you're OK back there, Vera?" Leona called to the back of the pickup where Vera sat with her back leaning up against the cab.

It was a slow bumpy ride through the pasture.

They delivered Johnny, unconscious but alive, to the Miller hospital and into the capable hands of the nurse on duty and Dr. Hendriks. The county's only doctor, Dr Hendriks had delivered Vera and had attended to her medical needs from vaccinations to a tonsillectomy, removal of warts, stitches on a number of occasions, a concussion, severe menstrual cramps, and had even pierced her ears.

Leona and Vera had the place to themselves as they settled into two of the five chairs in the waiting area of the small hospital.

"I didn't get down to coffee until late this morning." Leona leaned against Vera slightly as she talked.

"Wayne was finishing his second cup when I came in. Told me he'd seen dust thrown up by two vehicles. Early this morning. Looked to be along one of my section lines. Heading east."

"I didn't stay long." Leona glanced at Vera. "Thought I'd stop out at your place on my way home, ya know, to see about borrowing a post hole digger."

"Well I saw your car parked in the yard and could hear the dogs carrying on in the house." Leona rested her hand on Vera's arm as she continued her story.

"When you weren't in the house -- I let the dogs out just so ya know -- I started walking around the yard and saw some extra tire tracks down by barn and then some spots of blood." Leona stopped and blew her nose.

"Well, from what Wayne'd said, I knew which way to go. I found the gate open and followed the tire tracks in the grass." Leona's eyes were filling. "I'm just sorry I didn't get there sooner. I would have sent the scum who did this packing."

Vera put her arm around Leona's shoulder and gave her a squeeze. Vera knew that Leona, like most ranchers and farmers in the county, carried a rifle and knew how to use it. She was grateful Leona had not had an opportunity to confront the scum.

In about an hour Dr. Hendriks emerged from Johnny's room. "Your turn, Vera." She followed him back to a treatment room.

She was seated on the edge of an examining room table with Dr. Hendriks standing behind her. Leona's borrowed, now bloody, handkerchief lay on the floor. She was holding her hair forward so he could work on the gash.

"Hold still, Vera." He administered a shot of novocaine to deaden the area that needed stitches. While waiting for the anesthesia to take hold, he examined her swollen cheek. "You're going to have some bruising and it'll be sore for a few days but otherwise it looks OK."

He returned his attention to the deep gouge on the back of her head. She could smell the antiseptic he used to clean the wound.

"How's Johnny doing, Doc?" Vera asked the question as much to take her mind off the business going on behind her as to find out more about Johnny's health.

She could feel the tug of the needle as he pulled the skin together and sewed up the back of her head; she was grateful to feel no pain.

"Johnny should recover just fine. Fortunately, the bullet didn't hit his belly cavity. His blood pressure was low from losing so much blood, so he's getting a transfusion now along with IV fluids and antibiotics. He'll need to stay in the hospital a day or two, but all in all he should recover quickly."

"All done." He patted her shoulder. "Come back in a few days and I'll take out the stitches."

He scooted on his short round rolling-stool over to a metal cabinet in the corner of room, pulled out a bottle, filled a syringe and was waiting. "You're getting a tetanus shot."

"Seriously?! I think I've had one lately?" Defeated, Vera undid the top buttons of her jeans and inched the fabric down to expose the top of one cheek.

Vera felt a quick pinch.

Dr. Hendriks rolled around to give her a reassuring smile, closed the metal cabinet. "You'll be fine too."

He was at the door, holding it open for her.

"Thanks, Doc." She paused then asked. "When can I talk to Johnny?"

"He should be revived enough for you to talk with him in a couple hours." He walked her down the hall and back to Leona.

He leaned over and rested a reassuring hand on Leona's shoulder. "You doing OK, Leona?"

"Oh yeah, Doc, I'm fine." Leona gave a halfhearted smile then stood up and took Vera's elbow. "I'm going to get this girl home. She needs some rest."

## Chapter 28

Janet's troubled face looking out the window greeted him as James parked in front of the tribal police office.

She opened the door for him. "William didn't come home last night. The folks are worried."

He nodded. "OK, Janet, let me make a phone call and then I'll get out to look for him."

Again, Vera didn't answer her phone.

Janet was pacing between her desk and his, waiting for him to set down the phone. "James, I want to come with you. I have an idea of where he might be."

He paused to study her determined face. "OK, let's go."

"Pretty quiet." James drove slowly down main street. The two cars he passed were people he knew. He braked for a dog running across the road.

"Too quiet? Wonder what I'm missing?" James glanced at Janet staring through the passenger window, lost in her own thoughts. He let his drift too.

The rumors flying around the reservations came on the heels of longstanding complaints. Many people were tired of the way the federal government was treating the tribes. The way they had treated tribes historically. Tired of broken promises. Decades of broken promises. For some, it was time to take a stand.

Though he didn't have any answers or solutions for resolving the disputes between the federal government and the tribes, James was sure any violent actions initiated on the reservation would not end well for his people.

In the past couple of years, the complaints about the federal government had spilled over into resentment against the tribal governments. The feeling was that tribal government was representing the interests of the federal government over the interests of the people. Bitterness toward the tribal government was building.

James knew that over on Pine Ridge, people were fuming over the leadership of the tribal president. Dick Scott was seen as corrupt, that he made deals with the Feds that only benefited himself and his extended family, and that he rigged the elections so he kept winning the office of tribal president. It was widely known that Scott had even set up his own posse to enforce the laws as he saw fit. The Guardians of Oglala Nation -- GOONS -- Scott's private paramilitary group who did his bidding ruthlessly.

James and Sandra had talked about how Crow Creek and Lower Brule had been able to avoid those kinds of conflict. They agreed that a large part of the credit for keeping harmony on the reservations should go to the Elders, Howard Yellow-Knife, Evelyn Spotted Owl and the other older men and women who listened to complaints from tribal members with an open mind. The Elders encouraged conversations with all members of the tribe and tried to reach out to those most unhappy with the status quo.

Sandra strongly disagreed with James when their discussion turned to tensions between Natives living on reservations and their white neighbors living on adjacent ranches and in nearby towns.

It was James' opinion that tribal members living on Crow Creek and Lower Brule reservations, with their closer proximity to white ranchers and communities, had better working relationships with their white neighbors than did those members living on the more isolated Rosebud and Pine Ridge reservations. He pointed to their shared experiences. Native American kids attended nearby schools and played sports with white kids. Tribal ranchers, by necessity, often worked closely with their white neighbors. Shared fences and common issues bound their relationships in positive ways. Church was another place where Natives and whites came together.

James could see and hear the conversation in his mind, Sandra shaking her head and clucking at James' naivety. She thought he gave far too much credit to a supposed shared experience with their white neighbors. In her opinion, racist beliefs lived on with the whites in the area, just below the surface. Any cooperation with, and tolerance for, Natives continued as long as it benefited those white neighbors.

Janet pulled him back. She sat up to peer through the front window.

"Over the bridge on the south side there's an old fishing cabin along the old river road. I overheard William talking to someone on the phone a few days ago. I thought he was talking about meeting up to go fishing."

James glanced at her again. Her long black hair was tucked up into a baseball cap. Her mouth was set in a straight line.

She looked at James and said, "William doesn't always think things through."

James slowed the vehicle as Janet picked out the turn onto the unmarked road that dropped off the main river road. The track followed the river for a long half mile.

"It's the place where my grandfather used to take us to fish when we were little," she explained.

Not visible from the road, the old building was tucked up in a bend in the river and set up on the bank away from the shoreline to protect it against spring flooding.

James noticed the crumbling stone walls nearby, likely left from a time 150 years before when French fur traders gathered along the river to trade with the Indians.

Janet pointed. "There's his pickup."

She jumped out of the pickup before James could turn it off.

"William! Open up!" She pounded the door.

James hurried to step in front of her. "Hang on, Janet, we don't know who is in there."

When William pulled the door open a crack, she stepped back in front of James, her hands on her hips and her eyes narrowed to slits. "What're you doing, William?"

William gulped. "Geez, Janet."

"William, ya didn't come home last night. Mom's worried."
Janet could hear noises from inside. "Who else is in there,
William?"

Again James moved in front of her. "Hey William. How ya
doing?"

William was a skinny kid, no more than nineteen years
old. He had his hair pulled back with a band around his head. His
pants hung on his hips, his sweatshirt was stained and tattered.

"You should stay out of other people's business." William
gave Janet a withering look.

James pushed on the door and William reluctantly
stepped aside. James stopped short at the dark entrance. Janet,
on his heels, bumped into him.

The one room cabin smelled of fish and tobacco. In the
middle of the room, there was a tall wooden table used to clean
and fillet fish. A light bulb hung from the low ceiling over the
worn table. It's faint light reflected the dried fish scales
embedded in the surface. There were a couple of rickety wooden

chairs against the wall on either side of a window, one of which was occupied by Leonard. About the same age as William, Leonard had grown up in California but was sent to Fort Thompson to live with his grandparents a year ago.

"William, you're an idiot," Janet unloaded. "What're ya doing getting mixed up with this guy. Everyone knows he's here on the rez cause he's in trouble with the law in California."

"Will you guys just go away?" William pleaded. "Please."

Leonard stood up and looked out the window. Over his shoulder, he said, "William, they're here, man."

They heard tires on the road out front, a car motor turn off, followed by slamming doors.

James turned to William. "Who's here, William?"

Two men came barreling through the cabin door. James didn't recognize either one of them. The shorter of the two seemed to the leader. A cowboy hat pulled low over his eyes with a long braid down the back of his Che Guevara T-shirt, he appeared to be in his late twenties. He moved around to the window and looked out at the river road.

He turned back around to take a good look at James and Janet, then frowned.

"What the hell are they doing here?" He directed his question to William.

William glanced between James and the man at the window. "Sorry, Randall, they just showed up a couple of minutes ago."

"What're you doing here?" James directed his question to Randall.

Randall squinted to read the tribal police insignia on James' shirt and sneered. "Oh right, you're the protection on the rez. Protection for the feds."

Leonard and William had pushed themselves against the wall. James nudged Janet behind himself.

Nodding his head toward the man standing in the open doorway holding a rifle, James asked. "Why's this guy carrying? You guys with AIM?"

Randall stepped in close to James and hissed in his face. "You're an agent of the corrupt white federal government that has screwed the Natives for generations."

"Is that the party line coming from AIM?" James looked from one to the other. "You people are threatening the peace and safety of this community."

Randall continued with what seemed to James well rehearsed rant. "How are you not sick to death of the white government lying to you, breaking treaties, taking your land, trying to kill your language and taking over the education of your kids?"

"What would you know about it?" James demanded.

"I was born here. My people are from here," Randall shot back. "I've got a stake in this game."

"You know nothing about what goes on here." James shook his head. "Go back to where you're from and leave us alone."

"You got no backbone to stand up and take back what is ours." Randall quivered with anger. "AIM has a plan to end this lap dog tribal government and its collusion with the lying cheating white federal government."

"What is it you've got planned, Randall?" While keeping eye contact with Randall, James reached around and took Janet's elbow to inch them toward the door. "Something that will harm innocent people? How does that make you better than the white government you hate?"

James tried to push aside the stranger at the door. From behind him, he heard. "You're not going anywhere."

He was unprepared as the butt of a rifle slammed into his stomach. In the next moment, he collapsed into a ball on the floor. He couldn't breathe.

# Chapter 29

"Thanks, Leona. I won't be long." Moving carefully, Vera let herself out of Leona's pickup.

"Back in twenty minutes." Leona put her head out the window. "I'll just go pick up a few groceries while I'm here in town."

Vera gave her a quick smile and a slight nod. Vera had had to talk Leona into dropping her at the Sheriff's Office for a quick visit.

With the blood spots on Leona's shirt, Vera figured the story of Leona's morning -- and her own -- would be circulating through Miller within a few hours. Looking at her own appearance in the window of the front door, Vera knew she was carrying a good bit of the story herself, no sleeves on her blood-splotched sweatshirt, her jeans grimy and ripped in the knees, and her right cheek was swollen and turning black and blue. She'd pulled back her tangled hair to cover the stitches.

When she pushed open the front door and saw the expressions on the faces of Thelma and her new partner, Jerry, Vera knew she was right about her startling appearance.

"Oh my god! Are you OK?" Vera recognized Jerry, the other Hand County deputy. He bore a strong family resemblance to his older brother, though Vera never remembered Jerry's brother looking quite so put together. Jerry's uniform was pressed and his hair was neatly styled. And he smelled of cologne.

Jerry took her arm and led her to a comfortably padded chair. "Earl likes to share," Jerry explained.

"Good Lord, girl, looks like you've had yourself a rough morning." Thelma walked over for a close examine of Vera's face and head.

"Seriously, I'm OK." Vera tried to give her a reassuring look.

Thelma patted Vera's shoulder then returned to her desk, dug through a drawer until she found a bottle of aspirin.

She walked back to the sink in the corner, filled a glass of water and returned to Vera. "Here ya go, honey."

"Now, tell us what has happened to you." Jerry had pulled over a chair for himself and another for Thelma.

Vera recapped her morning. She then explained, without too many details, Johnny's part in the unfolding events in the county and on Crow Creek, centering on the crates of rifles that had been stored, first in Stella's shed, then in a cellar in Leona's pasture, and now apparently destined for Crow Creek. She described Johnny's partners -- Vince and Tattoos. She skimmed over the part of the story about being backhanded, hit over the head, and thrown down into the cellar. She quickly ended with Leona's rescue.

"That's crazy, Vera." Jerry had been hanging on to the story.

He dropped against the back of the chair and said with a sigh, "Nothing exciting ever happens around here."

Thelma had moved back to her chair behind her desk somewhere about mid-story, lit a cigarette and had begun taking notes.

"You said they were in two vehicles?" Thelma wanted to know. "Did you get the numbers off the plates?"

Vera wrote down the numbers and passed them to Thelma.

"Colorado? OK. I'll call the state patrol and have them keep a look out." She was already reaching for the phone. "You said a blue Ford pickup and an older Lincoln Continental, that right, Vera?"

"Yeah, but I doubt they would have gotten on the main roads. They seemed to know their way around the back roads."

Vera then circled around on the storyline to fill them in on encountering Johnny early Sunday morning in her yard. She linked him to Thomas Yellow-Knife and his death, passing along what she knew about how Thomas died.

"He died from eating candy?" Jerry confirmed the story of Thomas' cause of death.

"I want to get back to the hospital later this evening and talk with Johnny." Vera saw through the window that Leona had parked out in front. "Would you go over there and keep an eye on him, Jerry?"

"You bet, Vera." Jerry responded. "I'll head over there now."

Vera stood up slowly and headed out the front door.

"Take care, Vera." Thelma called after her.

Vera eased herself up into the cab of idling pickup. Leona let out the clutch and they headed back to Ree Heights.

Sitting at her aunt's kitchen table, Vera relaxed in the cool earthy smells of the old room, while Leona brought potato soup out of the fridge. A long counter extended the length of one wall; the tall windows above it framed geranium plants, bright with barn-red blooms and African Violets with softer shades of variegated purple and white blossoms. The windows faced east and looked out on gnarled old trees scattered across the yard and empty dog runs.

"Leona, remember Damnit?" Vera could feel the tension of the day lessen.

"Darn dog. Wouldn't come when I called him." Leona chuckled and stirred the soup. "'Til I figured out his name."

She set a bowl in front of Vera. "There now. Eat up."

Vera ate her supper and let Leona fuss.

"Vera, you've got to be more careful." Leona moved around the kitchen watering plants. "Goodness, I'm glad I followed those tracks up to the south pasture."

Vera knew Leona felt a responsibility for Wally and her since the death of their parents. Sitting in the calming quiet of Leona's kitchen, Vera realized she felt a reciprocal responsibility for her.

Vera finished the soup and felt a wave of exhaustion sweep over her. Leona, noticing, said, "OK then, Vera. Let's get you home."

## Chapter 30

It was end of the afternoon and hot. Swarms of flies settled and resettled on Vince as he waved them away. He sat in the shade of the old barn. It looked to Vince that the place had been deserted for years. Larson had driven them out here, said it'd make a good spot to hide the weapons. That was before he tried bullshitting them into thinking the deal was off. Be just like Larson to try to cut them out. Well he was in charge now.

Johnny and his niece, or whoever she was, were out of commission for a good long while. Vince doubted anyone would be looking for them in that hole.

They'd parked behind the old building hidden from view by anyone driving out on the county road. The doors of the car were open and he could hear Bobby snoring in the back seat.

They'd moved the pickup loaded with crates into the interior of the old barn and pulled the big doors closed.

The wind blew dust devils of powdery dry manure up into Vince's nostrils. He'd run out of cigarettes. He fucking hated waiting. They were supposed to meet up with the Indian at midnight down along the river. Only a few hours now and they would hand off the rifles, get paid, and get the hell out of this shithole. Vince threw his empty can on the pile and popped open another warm beer.

## Chapter 31

Vera woke up hot, sticky and confused. Her dogs were nosing her. After Leona dropped her off, she had lain down on the couch to rest.

She sat up carefully, her head throbbing, as the events of the day resurfaced. Her fingers gently tapped the stitches on the back of her scalp then she tentatively felt her bruised cheek.

"Hey, pups. What a day, huh?" Vera rubbed the fur behind the ears of each dog, then pushed herself up and opened windows around the little house. The evening air felt refreshing. She took a long hot shower.

In her experience with city hospitals, Vera knew visiting hours were set in stone. She suspected the Miller Hospital would be different. She parked in a diagonal slot in front. Only two other cars in the row. There was no one at front desk so she walked down the central corridor looking for the nursing staff.

Louise Lake, an old family friend, was working the evening shift. Louise pulled her into a warm, fragrant hug.

"Vera, honey." Vera immediately teared up. Charlie had been her mom's favorite perfume too.

"You doing all right?" Louise had her at arm's length to examine her face. "You've got a shiner."

Louise's pump arms pushed at the bands of her uniform sleeves as she turned Vera around. "Let's have a look at those stitches."

"Dr. Hendriks has done a fine job," she declared. "You'll be right as rain in no time, Vera."

Louise studied her face for a minute more. "Guess you are here to see Johnny?"

"You think he's up to company? I need to ask him some questions." Louise led Vera down the hall to Johnny's room.

Before she went in, Vera turned to Louise. "I don't see Jerry? Thought he'd be here tonight. Johnny is under arrest or will be as soon as I read him his Miranda rights."

"Oh Jerry's been here. He should be right back. His mother called for him about a half hour ago." Louise gave a little giggle. "You remember his mother, Vera?"

Vera glanced at Louise who was still chuckling. "I do remember Jerry's mother. It's part of the reason I didn't date his brother."

Louise stopped in front of Johnny's door and whispered, "What the heck is Johnny Larson doing back in these parts, anyway?"

"Oh right. Guess you knew Johnny?" Vera had forgotten that Louise might have known Johnny.

"Knew of him," Louise chuckled. "He had a bit of reputation."

"Oh? A reputation? With the ladies ya mean?" Vera looked at Louise and prompted, "Apparently Mom and Johnny dated for a few months before Dad came back from the Navy?"

"Oh gosh, Vera honey, that was a long time ago."

Louise swung the door open and led the way to Johnny's bedside.

"Johnny, you feel up for some company?" Louise inspected the fluids bag hooked up to Johnny.

"Oh sure." Johnny grunted and turned his head toward Vera. "I figured you'd be back."

From the door, and in her nurse voice, Louise said, "I'll be back in a bit to kick you out, Vera, Johnny still needs some rest."

The window was about a quarter of the way open and Vera could hear kids out on the street. Shouts over whose turn it was. Dogs barking. A cool breeze was just starting to lift the curtains. The shift to an evening climate had begun.

"Guess we have some unfinished business?" Johnny blinked his eyes and focused on Vera's face.

"Yes, we do." Vera pulled up a chair next the bed and opened the notebook she'd brought along.

He'd been cleaned up and shaved, and smelled better. His curly hair was cut short, his cheeks were mottled, his skin along his jawline sagged making the cleft in his chin more pronounced.

"You are under arrest for the transportation of illegal weapons with the intent to sell. And for stealing gas." She read him his rights while Johnny stared at the ceiling.

He rolled his head toward her. Tears were in his eyes.

Surprised, she asked, "Are you in pain, Johnny."

She stood up. "Should I call Louise?"

"He was dead when I found him." Tears were now slipping down his cheeks.

She assumed she knew the answer, but asked, "Who do ya mean, Johnny?"

"Thomas. I went out to the ranch where he was working to spend some time with him and I found him dead on the floor of the barn." Johnny stared at the ceiling again, his face pulled down with grief. He was quiet, seemed to be lost in thought.

"How did you know him?" Vera asked gently. "Why were you there to see him?"

Aware again of her presence, he said, "Oh Vera, there's a lot you don't know about me."

"Yeah. I'm guessing that's true." Vera leaned back in the chair and waited.

"Thomas was my son. I didn't know about him until a couple of years ago. I only met him for the first time three months ago."

Vera gave a low whistle. "Thomas was your son?"

Johnny glanced at her. "I met his mother the summer of 1957 when I was living in Denver. I was between jobs for a few months. I left the area in the fall. I went to work for the U.S. government delivering guns to the South Vietnamese."

Vera looked up from her notebook. "Guns seem to be a theme in your life."

Johnny either didn't hear or ignored the sarcasm in her voice.

He continued, "I know I've screwed up a lot of things in my life but I wanted to do right by Thomas."

"We'll come back to Thomas." Vera stood up and started to pace. "What were you and your partners planning to do with the crates of guns? Do you have a buyer?"

"I met Vince Blazo and Bobby Durant two years ago when I moved back to Denver." Johnny didn't try to follow Vera's movement. "I had access to weapons and they had the connections. We made some money selling to gangs in northern Mexico."

Vera was at the end of his bed.

She turned to face him. "Really? You continued your career of gun running in this country?"

Johnny finished, "About three months ago I set up a deal to sell weapons to a faction group of Natives operating out of Crow Creek. Told Vince and Bobby I'd get up here and hide the weapons since I knew my way around. The plan was for them to come up a few days later and help with the hand off."

"My God, Johnny, you brought those men up here? And you gave them a tour of your old hometown?" Her voice had risen with the questions. "Where are they now? Where are the guns now?"

His focus seemed to be on the tree branches moving in the top of the window as he provided her answers. "We were staying in Kadoka in a motel off the interstate. Vince and Bobby probably left there though. They might be holed up in an abandoned property off the road where highway 34 turns to go to Fort Thompson."

"Who on the reservation wanted to buy the guns?" Vera felt her heart sink. She needed to talk to James.

"I worked through a contact from Denver. Man by the name of Randall. I'm guessing he has ties to AIM. They'd be the only ones with enough money to buy that many weapons."

He turned to look at her directly. "The weapons will be handed over tonight. Somewhere down along the river."

"I've got to go." Vera stood up, headed toward the door, then turned back around. "How'd ya know where to find Wally? "

"Your Dad showed me the property a couple of years ago after I'd moved back to the states. He and Elsa had just bought it for Wally. I'd come up to visit them, had a business idea for Everett. Turns out he wasn't interested." His voice faded with the end of the explanation.

She pressed her lips together, let a puff of air escape her nose, and nodded her head slightly.

Then she asked, "Why'd you steal his rifle?

"I needed it. Figured things were going to get dicey with Vince and Bobby." Vera gave him a last look then pulled the door open to leave.

"Wait." Johnny's voice pulled her around. "How did Thomas die?"

"Thomas died from an anaphylaxis reaction." Johnny studied her face as she continued. "The coroner said that Thomas must have been allergic to nuts and that the candy he had eaten had caused a severe reaction in his body."

Johnny had a look of shock, disbelief, and horror. "Oh my god. I killed my own boy."

She gulped in a breath. "You gave him the candy."

She wasn't sure he heard her say as she left the room, "His funeral will be early tomorrow morning."


## Chapter 32

James groaned as he was pulled to his feet.

Janet took his other arm and helped him stand. She supported him as they were pushed toward the door.

"Ray, you and Leonard get them outta here. There's another old fishing cabin about quarter mile further down the river. Move his truck down there too."

Randall turned to William. "Isn't that what you told me?" Then added, "You're staying here with me."

James stumbled in the growing darkness and gasped with the pain.

He glanced at Janet's face; she looked shocked and scared. He whispered, "I'm OK. It'll be all right."

"Get in." Ray directed James toward one vehicle.

He looked at Janet. "You ride with Leonard."

Janet helped James into the cab of the truck then walked over to James' pickup where Leonard waited and climbed in.

Dusk was falling as the pickup bounced over a trail in the weeds along the river. James gingerly held his stomach over the bumps. He looked over at Ray in the driver's seat. He had a stocky build with workout biceps straining his T-shirt.

"Who are you and Randall meeting tonight?" James prodded somewhat breathlessly as he was having difficulty taking deep breaths. "This got anything to do with a shipment of rifles?"

Ray didn't look at James as he commented, "The white man forced us on the reservations. Then forced us off our lands again with policies aimed at disempowering us." Ray looked out across the river. "We're here to reclaim our lands, our government and our education."

James frowned and asked, "What claim do you have to the tribe, to this land?"

"My folks were born here. They were forced into the white man's boarding schools back east. They were just little kids." Ray spoke in a measured tone. "They never returned. Never saw their families again. Never spoke their language again. Never practiced their traditions again."

James saw the cabin up ahead.

"My folks're both dead. Drank themselves to death. They tried to make a go of it in Omaha after leaving Carlisle. I grew up in a run-down neighborhood near the packing plant where my dad worked until they fired him."

James glanced at him as he finished his story. "I'm doing this in their memory."

He brought the pickup to a stop; Leonard pulled up alongside it. James climbed out carefully.

Ray pointed with his gun to the falling-down shack. "Both of you. Get in there."

No door on the ancient structure. James gripped the doorframe but tripped over the threshold. Janet caught his arm. The roof had caved in on one side leaving a partial shelter the size of a closet.

James turned to Ray who stood outside. "Listen, Janet's not a threat to you. Let her go."

Leonard came in with baling twine.

"Really, Leonard, is this what you want to do?" James tried to meet his eye.

Ray's voice came from near his vehicle. "Hurry up in there, Leonard."

Seated on the dirt floor and backed up against a wall, wrists and ankles bound, James and Janet watched the last of the daylight play on the river through the door opening. They heard the truck motor disappear.

Two hours later Janet nudged James gently. "Hey, James, wake up. I hear a vehicle."

James tried to move his body but felt a deep stab of pain. He figured he may have a cracked rib.

They heard a motor turn off, footsteps, then were caught in the beam of a flashlight.

"Where's my boy, James?" James recognized the voice.

"Heard you might be on the rez." James looked up at his wife.

"You heard right. I'm here to get my son." Martha's demands came through the light. "Not planning on staying. I'll get Lucas and we'll get out of here. This is no place for him to grow up."

"The hell you will." James tried again to move.

"I've been to the house. Where is he?"

"You left him and me a year ago and haven't bothered to call or visit in all that time." James pulled hard on his rope at his wrists.

"Did you take him out to your parents? I'll just bet you did." Martha chuckled. "Guess I'll take a drive out there tonight. They can't stop me from taking custody of my own son."

The beam of light disappeared. A minute later they heard the motor turn over.

## Chapter 33

Rumbling skies accompanied Vera back to Ree Heights. Rain drops dotted her windshield as she pulled up in the yard.

The rain let loose as she ran into the house with dogs on her heels.

Lightening cracked while the dogs bounced around her legs.

She leaned over to rub them down. "OK. OK. I'm home."

She turned on the light in the kitchen and looked outside at the sky that had turned an almost bright yellow-green color. She heard the hail hit the roof then watched the ice balls slam against the ground. The noise was deafening for a couple of minutes and then just as quickly it stopped, replaced by rain. The lights in the kitchen flickered and went out.

Standing in the growing darkness, Vera picked up the phone. The line was dead.

The rain drummed on the roof as she made a decision.

"I'm leaving you guys again. You'll be fine." She filled their bowls with dog food and water.

She dug into the back of the coat closet for her dad's rain slicker and his old felt hat, shoved a couple of apples into her pockets and headed out into the rain.

The rain had quit by the time Vera drove into Fort Thompson. She wasn't surprised to see that there were no lights on at the tribal offices. She drove on to James' house.

She stepped out of the car into the wet grass and up onto the front porch. No lights on at his house either. She knocked and waited.

She opened the door, calling as she moved into the house. The house was stuffy from being closed up for the day. She walked through the house to the kitchen, then returned to the small living room.

She didn't know where to look for James. Hopefully he would return home soon. She turned on a lamp, opened the windows, then sat down on the couch. Her head ached. She could hear bugs hitting the screen door, attracted by the light.

## Chapter 34 -- early Wednesday morning

Janet's head had dropped on James' shoulder and he could hear her even breathing. He'd been watching the sky lighten for an hour or so. Ground fog hovered above the marshy banks of the river. Any small movement caused him considerable pain, but he'd gotten his wrists out of the rope that bound them without disturbing Janet.

He heard footsteps and heavy breathing. Within a couple of minutes William's head came around the corner of the doorway.

"Glad to see ya, William." James whispered.

William spoke softly. "I snuck away but need to get right back."

Janet was instantly awake. "Oh thank god, you came to help us."

William was at work on the rope at Janet's wrists. "I left them sleeping but they'll be awake soon."

"Who's at the cabin? Is Martha there?" James asked.

He glanced at James then finished untying the rope. "She left a few hours ago. Told Randall she was staying long enough to get what she wanted and then was leaving the state."

William sat down beside Janet in the narrow space and stared out over the river. "Two more AIM guys showed up. Randall's pissed. Whoever was supposed to deliver the rifles hasn't shown up yet."

He looked at Janet. "I'm sorry about this."

She looked at him then back across the river.

James responded. "We'll get out of here and get back to town for help. You better get yourself back to the cabin."

William slipped out quickly. They heard his footsteps for only a moment then it was quiet.

James asked. "Janet, will you see if the keys are in my truck?"

When she left, he got to his knees, clutched at the door frame and tried to get to his feet. He felt sick to his stomach and sat back down.

She returned a couple minutes later. "They're not in the truck."

She could hear his raspy breathing. "Listen, James, you aren't in any shape to move, much less walk. I'm going to run to town."

"Hmm." James breathed in as deeply as he could and let out a long sigh. His shoulders sagged. The sky was getting lighter by the minute. "Climb to the top of the hill. Probably it'll be OK to run on that road. Duck in the weeds if you see a vehicle. Go down to the old bridge to cross the river."

"I'll be fine, James." She took a long look at his face that was now more visible with the increasing daylight. His skin was ashen and there were dark rings under his eyes.

"I'll be back with help." And she was out the door.

"Be careful."

## Chapter 35

"What're ya doin? James looked down at her, one eyebrow raised.

"Oh nothing." Vera stood close to him. She looked up at him and grinned.

"That's kinda weird, ya know. You smelling me." He pulled her into his chest for a hug.

She lay still as the dream dissolved.

They'd laughed, years ago, when she used to stand next to him and tell him that she loved the smell of him.

That was a long time ago, she reminded herself.

Vera sat up slowly, touched the back of her head gently as she looked around in the early morning light. Her head throbbed.

She stood up from the couch, turned off the lamp and moved to stand at the screen door. She could hear birds in the trees out near the barn and a rooster in a yard nearby. She saw only her vehicle in the yard.

Vera found aspirin in James' bathroom and took two, then took a third one. She looked in the mirror at her wild hair more red than brown this morning. She carefully worked her hair into a braid then threw water on her face. The bruise on her cheek had darkened to a solid black and blue. She decided against using the toothbrush standing in the holder.

In the kitchen she found coffee grounds and matches. She ran water in the coffee pot then lit the gas under it. While she waited for the water to boil, she heard insistent, loud meowing. James' cat was at the kitchen screen door with a mouse.

"Good work, kitty, but you aren't bringing that thing into the house."

She added grounds to the pot, let it boil up and settle back down a couple of times, then turned down the flame.

She carried the steaming cup to the phone in the front hall.

Thelma answered on the first ring. "Where have you been, Vera?"

She sounded shaken. "I tried calling you last night. A few times."

Vera set her coffee mug down on the hall table. "What's going on?"

"Johnny left the hospital last night. When Louise looked in on him about 9:30 he was gone."

"Gone? Where was Jerry?"

"Jerry had to run out on an errand." Thelma's voice got tighter. More abrupt. "He was only gone for a few minutes. Anyway when he got back Johnny was gone."

"He couldn't have gotten far? He was hurt."

Thelma hesitated. "Well, that's the thing."

"What's the thing?" Vera held onto her frustration.

"He stole Ted Poindexter's car."

Vera paused. "Because Ted left the keys in the ignition."

"Well, yes." Thelma finished in a rush. " Anyway, Jerry has been driving around most of the night. He hasn't found Johnny or Ted's car."

Vera let out a long sigh. "OK. Ask Jerry to come down to Fort Thompson. Earl too if he's around. I think I may need some backup. Tell them to come to the tribal offices."

"I'll tell them." Thelma hung up.

Vera stood again at the screen door and finished her coffee.

## Chapter 36

There was a hushed feeling in Betty's yard where a half dozen vehicles were parked. Vera angled her Bug into an available space and quietly closed the car door. The windows in the house were open and she could hear a rhythmic chanting and drumming, low and steady.

An older woman came to the door and waved her in. Evelyn Spotted Owl introduced herself, gave Vera a sad smile, and walked her to where Betty was seated. People were sitting and standing all around her, talking quietly. Vera guessed that many of the people gathered in the room had stayed with Betty through the night while others had arrived earlier this morning to be on hand to go with her to the cemetery.

On the other side of the room, Vera saw a circle of folding chairs, each occupied, surrounding a plain pine coffin.

Along one wall of the room tables were filled with food, casseroles, cookies, macaroni and jello salads, and coffee to drink.

The kitchen beyond hummed with hushed activity.

On the walls were pictures, among them, Vera saw Thomas' high school graduation picture.

Evelyn pulled up a chair for her, close to Betty.

Vera nodded her thanks.

Leaning toward the older woman, Vera spoke quietly. "Betty, I know we haven't met, and I so wish we could be meeting in happier circumstances. I'm Vera Carlson with the Hand County Sheriff's Department."

Betty patted her hand. "Thank you for coming by."

Evelyn brought Vera a cup of coffee and a slice of rhubarb bread. The tangy bread was delicious and brought back memories. Her mom had made many batches of rhubarb bread each spring when the plant in her garden started producing. The room and Betty's sad face had started to blur in her vision. She cleared her throat and wiped at the corner of her eyes.

"Betty, I've spent some time with the man who came by looking for Thomas last Friday. His name is Johnny Larson. He believed he was Thomas' father. He only recently learned of Thomas' existence and had wanted to build a relationship with your nephew."

Betty looked in her lap. "Yes, James told me about this man. The man who gave Thomas the candy."

"Yes, it was a tragic mistake." Vera spoke to Betty's bowed head. "In the little time Johnny spent with Thomas, he found so many qualities to admire about him."

Vera continued, "Johnny told me how much Thomas loved you and how he wanted to be a help for you."

242

She looked up briefly, tears in her eyes. "Thanks for telling me good things about my boy."

In the corner of the room, seated around a large drum, the drummers communicated the grief held in the room. It seemed to Vera a song both universal and eternal.

"I know you are leaving soon for the burial." She squeezed Betty' hand gently and stood up to leave.

An older man waited for Vera at the front door. "I'm Howard, Betty's brother." He held out his hand. "Thanks for coming by this morning. James said you were working with him."

"Howard, good to meet you. Vera Carlson, sheriff's deputy." Vera looked up into warm brown eyes. "So sorry for your loss."

"It's been hard on Betty. Hard on all of us. Losing Thomas." Howard's shoulders were bent and his long braid was silver.

She asked softly, "Howard, I'm wondering if you've seen James?"

Howard took her elbow and moved with her out the front door and down into the yard.

Vera saw his worried look.

Howard explained, "I thought he would have stopped by last night and for sure this morning. But he hasn't come by."

Vera's brow furrowed as she looked across the yard. "I drove down last night when I couldn't get ahold of him on the phone. He wasn't at his house." She looked up again at Howard. "I waited there but he hasn't shown up."

"James told me that he was worried about some guns coming onto the reservations." Howard sighed heavily.

Vera turned to Howard. "Johnny Larson, the man who believes he is Thomas' father, came to the area with two partners. They made a deal to sell weapons to a group who may be associated with AIM."

Howard nodded.

Vera continued, "He had a falling out with those partners and was in the hospital in Miller last night. No doubt his partners are planning to finish what they started."

She finished up in a hurry. "Johnny left the hospital last night. Maybe he's had a change of heart and wants back in the deal? It was supposed to go down last night."

Vera's voice quivered. "The thing is I don't know where to look for them. I'm worried that James might be there -- wherever they are."

"Can you wait here?" Howard went back into the house.

He returned with a young man. "This is Robert. He might be able to help."

Robert kicked at the ground then looked up at Howard then at Vera. "William and the new kid Leonard have been hanging around together. They talk about how they are going to bring some changes to the reservation."

Robert looked at Howard. "I didn't think they were serious, Uncle. Mostly bored, I thought. But maybe they're mixed up in this?"

Robert looked at Vera and back at Howard. "I might know where they are."

Howard responded. "Vera, meet us at the tribal offices in about an hour?"

He laid a hand gently on Robert's shoulder. "Let's get back with the others. It's time to go to the cemetery."


## Chapter 37

Vera couldn't remember the last time she'd been in Kadoka. She pulled up in front of the only operating motel in town.

A gaggle of dogs -- large and small, short haired and long -- came around to sniff her legs as she entered the small office. Vera looked over the counter at a man seated at the desk writing in a ledger. He looked up through the bifocals resting on the end of his nose. His shirt buttoned snugly around his large belly.

Vera introduced herself and her role as sheriff's deputy.

"I'm looking for three men who may have stayed here in the past three or four nights."

"Yeah, lady. Three men stayed here over the weekend. Checked out yesterday if ya want to call it that. Trashed the room and left." He bent his head back to his work.

"I'd like the key to the room to take a look around."

"Sure. It's room number twelve." Without getting up, he slid the key across the counter.

Vera sidled backwards out the front door to avoid letting the dogs out.

She walked along the cracked sidewalk in front to the last room at the end of line of doors in the rundown building. She knocked on the door then used the key to let herself in. The room smelled strongly of stale cigarette smoke and beer.

Leaving the door open for light and ventilation, she looked under the bed and through drawers in the bedside tables, pulled back the curtains and glanced in the bathroom, then she stepped back outside.

Around the side of the building, she found Wally's rifle was propped up against the wall.

## Chapter 38

Howard watched Thomas' casket being lowered into the ground. The ceremony had been brief, with the community of family and friends there to support Thomas on his journey to the afterlife.

Traditionally, foods and tools were provided for the dead to make that journey. Gifts for Thomas -- a letter jacket, pocket knife, fishing hook, a book -- had been placed inside the coffin when it was opened a last time before burial.

Howard stood near Robert as the funeral reached its end.

Robert's slumped shoulders carried the pain he was experiencing. He'd stayed on through the long night and had helped carry the coffin holding Thomas' body to its final resting spot. Now he wiped his eyes and stared at the wooden box in the earth.

Thomas and Robert had been good friends. They had a shared experience of living with an older relative, Thomas with his great-aunt Betty, and Robert with his grandmother. Evelyn had raised Robert after his parents moved away to the city to look for jobs. They sent money to help with the care of Robert and they got back to the reservation from time to time.

The young boys had filled a void for Howard after his wife died. They'd shown an interest in learning the history and traditions of the tribe. Howard had spent many hours with them, telling them stories, showing them how to use the old tools, teaching them the rituals. Howard was grateful knowing the boys would carry the customs and rituals, traditions and language, forward into the next generation.

Howard spoke gently to Robert who stared down into the grave. "Thomas would be glad for your respect and kindness to his aunt."

Robert looked up at him. "I miss him, Uncle."

"We'll hold Thomas in our memories." Howard responded quietly. "He will be with us in spirit."

Robert had glanced again at Howard. He looked worried.

"Uncle, there are rumors that outsiders have come onto the reservation to make trouble."

Howard nodded slowly. "I've heard the talk about those people coming here, turning distrust into anger."

Howard had felt the cohesion of the tribe in the past days, in the way so many had come together for Thomas -- and for Betty. He felt certain that the community would not be open to aggressive actions by outsiders.

"Let me talk to these people." Howard leaned on Robert's arm as he moved across the uneven ground toward Robert's vehicle. "Let's go to meet the sheriff's deputy."

## Chapter 39

Johnny stood back in the stand of scrub oaks to watch. The stone church and graveyard rested on the crest of a bluff overlooking the river.

He'd left the stolen car parked on a dirt road below the bluff and walked up the steep hill. The wound in his side had begun to seep blood.

He saw a priest, white robe flapping in the wind, standing at the top of coffin. The ceremony at Thomas' gravesite was over quickly.

He silently offered his own good bye to a son he had only recently met, then turned and slid down the hill to the car.

He had work to do. His partners were counting on him to deliver the weapons and he intended to finish the job.

## Chapter 40

Ray came out to stand with Randall who stood watching the sun break over the riverbank on the far side.

Ray breathed in deeply. The small cabin was crowded with sleeping bodies and smelled like it.

"Fuck it," Randall's growled. "Where the hell is Larson?"

Ray lowered his voice. "You heard them. The two AIM guys who came in last night. Said to be cool. Said that it'd work out. Gotta be patient."

"I'm sick of waiting." Once again a white man was holding him back, delaying his future.

"Unbelievable." Randall's voice registered his disgusted. "These people don't seem to know their own history."

He pointed with his chin to the town of Crow Creek in the distance. "They're willing to let the feds jerk them around. They've got no fight."

"Keep an eye on William." Randall turned to Ray. "Ever since his sister showed up with the cop, he's been acting a little flaky."

They walked back toward the cabin.

Randall could see Martha sleeping in the car. Alone. She must have come back in the night -- without her son. No doubt she'd chew into her husband when she woke up.

Before going back inside, he looked out over the river, then up at the bridge a half mile awhile.

"Fuck." He spit.

## Chapter 41

Vera stepped out of her car at the same time that Howard and Robert pulled up.

Robert was out of the truck. "What're you doing here?"

Janet sat on the step, her face flushed and sweaty.

Howard climbed down more slowly. "Janet, are you OK?"

Janet stood up, held onto the railing. "James is hurt. He's in an old cabin near the river."

Robert asked. "You ran here? From there?"

She glanced at Robert, nodded, then continued, directing herself to Howard. "There are people, outsiders, at another cabin nearby. They're waiting for weapons to be delivered."

Just then another vehicle arrived. This one carried Earl and Jerry.

Vera introduced everyone then brought Earl and Jerry up to speed. "Janet's been telling us about the situation down at a cabin on the river. James is being held there." Vera looked to Janet. "And there are armed men waiting for weapons to be delivered."

Earl asked Vera, "We're assuming these are the weapons Johnny and his partners brought up for sale on the reservation?"

Earl looked to Howard. "The reservation is under federal jurisdiction. The Hand County Sheriff Department could offer assistance as requested."

"Yes, we need some help." Howard replied then looked around the group. "I want to try to talk with these people. They are frustrated and want to show their strength but violence isn't the answer."

Janet and Howard rode in Robert's truck. Vera, riding with Earl and Jerry, followed them.

Earl drove. He looked in the rearview mirror at Vera who sat in the backseat. "Heard you had a rough day yesterday? That's quite a shiner you got."

Vera caught Earl's eye in the mirror. "I'm doing OK."

From his passenger seat in the front, Jerry turned around to face Vera. "Sorry to let Johnny slip away last night."

Vera looked out the window and didn't respond.

Earl glanced at her again and cleared his throat. "Vera, the reason Jerry wasn't at the hospital last night was because he'd gone to check on Wally."

Vera frowned and looked directly at Jerry. "You were checking on Wally? What's going on?"

"He's OK." Jerry studied her face. "You maybe didn't know that Wally and I went to high school together? We weren't especially close in those years. But since he's gotten back from Vietnam, he's needed some support. I work at the Miller VFW running a veterans group. My degree is in psychology and counseling. Earl hired me as a deputy so I can pay the bills."

Jerry continued with the story. "Wally called last night, upset. Thought he'd lost a new puppy he'd just gotten. We found the little guy asleep in the back seat of one of cars in the garage."

Vera let out a long breath and gave Jerry a weak smile. "Thanks for going over there."

Jerry furrowed his brow. "I didn't stay long, but long enough for Johnny to make an exit."

"He's slippery." She sighed deeply, her head was aching again.

Earl followed Robert's pickup over the bridge. He braked abruptly as the vehicle in front of him made a sharp turn down along the shore.

Robert slowed to a near crawl, then stopped. Earl parked behind him.

Vera could see Janet pointing to the top of the bluff. She looked up and saw James slowly moving down the hill.

Robert got out of his truck and walked back to the car. He leaned over and said in a hushed voice through the open windows, "Janet says the cabin is less than a quarter mile away. When we drive out from under these trees we'll be in view of it and them of us. Howard wants to go in on his own. He thinks he can get them to listen." Robert didn't sound convinced.

Janet got out of the truck and Howard moved over into the driver's seat.

Janet walked back to stand near Robert. "I'm worried about Howard. The men at the cabin are dangerous."

"I couldn't change his mind. He wants to talk to them." Robert stared at the back of Howard's hunched shoulders behind the wheel.

They all watched as the truck slowly moved ahead and disappeared into the trees.

All was quiet as they waited. Vera looked up the hillside again for James but he was gone from sight.

"OK, long enough. Pile in." Earl urged. "We need to move in closer."

When Earl brought the car through the trees and into sight of the cabin, Vera saw a man in the doorway of the cabin, holding a rifle. Howard stood a short distance in front of him. Vera saw a movement in the shadow of the cabin and spotted James behind the old building.

Vera saw the man with the rifle look at their approaching vehicle then call over his shoulder. Immediately the space around him was filled with more rifles, all pointed in their direction.

Vera heard Howard as he slowly moved toward the armed men who had moved out into the yard to stand with Randall. "Let's talk." She heard the old man say. "We don't need violence. This can be solved peacefully. Lower your guns."

She saw James step around the cabin to stand next to Howard.

In the clearing Vera and the others slowly got out of the car. They moved to stand behind the vehicle as they watched and listened to the drama unfold in front of them.

"Old man. Get in your truck and leave." Randall was in charge. "We are way past talking."

At that point, two young men who seemed to be struggling over a rifle pushed out of the cabin and into the middle space between the Randall's armed group and Howard and James.

Vera heard Janet gasp. "That's William. And Leonard."

Vera watched as the two fought for control of the gun.

Suddenly the rifle discharged and Howard crumpled to the ground.

"Uncle. You've been hit." Robert broke from the group and ran to the older man.

James knelt beside Howard, quickly finding and applying pressure to the wound.

Just then, someone in the armed group shouted and pointed to the bridge.

Looking up and squinting against the early morning sun, Vera saw the old blue Ford loaded with crates of rifles lumber up onto the bridge and slowly make its way across.

Vera shaded her eyes and stepped out into the open for better look.

As he got closer Vera could see Johnny through the front window of the old truck. He was focused with a determined look on his face.

"Well, looks like he's here with the delivery," she said to Earl who had come to stand by her.

Neither she nor Earl took their eyes off the truck. "Yeah. Looks like." He replied.

It had gotten very quiet along the river as they all watched the truck with the weapons approach.

Vera heard someone in the group at the cabin say, "Finally, he shows up."

With even more speed Johnny crested the middle of the bridge.

Vera frowned and murmured, "What's he doing?"

Everyone in the two groups watched as Johnny pointed his truck toward the low cable strung along the side of the bridge. Then with even greater acceleration, drove it off the edge.

The old Ford hit the water hood-first.

They all watched as the truck disappeared from sight, the weight of the guns pulling the vehicle with Johnny in it to the bottom of the river.

There was a collective gasp followed by a stunned silence.

## Chapter 42

Everyone along the shoreline stood immobilized for a few minutes trying to comprehend what they just witnessed. Slowly there was movement, a rearrangement of the dynamic.

Vera watched as, almost immediately, the four members of the AIM group loaded up in their vehicle and drove away from the cabin leaving Randall behind.

"You coming along?" Randall had directed his question to a woman who'd only just emerged from the cabin. She was tall and slim with long black hair.

"Nothing left here." He added as he looked around.

Vera heard the woman as she walked up to James. "Don't think you've heard the last of me. I'll be back for my boy."

Then she got in the car with Randall. Following the first vehicle, they drove down the river road away from the scene of would-be rebellion that had sunk with the guns.

With Howard loaded into the cab and leaning heavily on James, Robert steered the truck slowly over the bumps. Janet, William and Leonard rode in the bed of the truck as they headed for town.

Vera stood looking at the truck as it passed by. James caught her eye and gave a brief nod of his head. She lifted her hand slightly in response.

Earl's question brought her back. "Let's see if we can find Johnny's partners?"

She looked at him and Jerry then squinted her eyes. "Hmm. I have an idea about where they might be if they are still around."

They started back across the bridge. Earl stopped at the point where Johnny's truck had plunged into the river. The low guard rail, now torn, had done little to slow down the heavy vehicle.

They got out of the car and carefully looked over the edge of the bridge into the river.

Vera stared into the river's strong current. Small birds were dipping and diving under the bridge. "It's as if it didn't happen."

"Except we all saw it happen and we'll never forget it." Earl responded as he stared at the water's surface.

"It's a story that will have a life of its own," Jerry commented, also mesmerized by the swirling eddies below.


Vera directed Earl to the deserted property Johnny had mentioned to her from his hospital bed, halfway between Ree Heights and Fort Thompson.

Vera knew the property well from the summer, years ago, when she and James would meet, seeking some privacy, hidden from the prying eyes of their communities.

Weathered and gray, the old house she remembered was tilting even more precariously, the glass broken out of its windows and the front steps collapsed. Down a slope from the house sat an equally ancient barn but in better condition. Behind the barn they found Ted's stolen car and the Lincoln driven by the gun dealers.

"Jerry, there's a handgun under the seat." Earl reached into his front shirt pocket and pulled out bullets.

"I carry this piece, but this is first time I've used it in years." He loaded the gun.

With his gun drawn and leading the way, Earl moved tentatively into the dim space of the building. Vera and Jerry followed close behind him.

Peering over the first horse stall, they looked over the top rail and saw a balding man with a big gut, his arms tied behind him. His ankles were also tied and his shoes were missing.

She snorted and mumbled, "Nice work, Johnny."

She looked down at him, tilted her head to one side and asked. "How's it going there, Vince?"

He erupted, "Where the hell is goddam Larson?"

There was a whine from a nearby stall. "Yeah, where's Johnny? He took off with his truck and the guns and left us here."

"These the guys we're looking for, Vera?" Earl confirmed the obvious.

She followed him back out to his car, where he popped the trunk and pulled out handcuffs, manacles, baling wire, and duct tape.

"Like how you come prepared," Vera commented.

"Ready for any eventuality." Earl winked at her.

"Let's start with Tattoos," she suggested.

Together they entered the stall holding Bobby; Earl handcuffed his wrists and manacled his stockinged feet. Vera took an elbow and began to shuffle him to the car while Earl and Jerry moved on to Vince.

"Johnny showed up here earlier, huh?" she asked Bobby as he inched along.

"Johnny came out with coffee and donuts late last night," he explained. "Said he had gotten outta the hospital."

Coming out of the barn, Bobby blinked hard in the bright sun. "Said things had changed for him and that he intended to go ahead with the sale."

"Is that right?" she asked as she propelled him to Earl's car. "How'd you guys get tied up?"

She opened a backdoor of the car and guided Bobby into the backseat. He continued with his story. "We was drinking coffee and eating donuts when things got blurry. Next thing I know I'm waking up all tied up in that stall. Looks like Johnny took off with the guns. Looks like he cut us out of the deal." He looked up at her.

"Well, geez Bobby, that's a lot of bad luck." Vera rolled down the window, closed the car door then pulled Bobby's handcuffed wrists out of the window. Using the baling wire she secured the handcuffs to the outside door handle.

She turned to see Earl and Jerry escorting Vince out of the barn.

"The son of bitch Larson shows up with some story about changing his mind. Looks to me like he two-timed us -- selling the guns on the rez for himself -- cutting us out. I'll find his sorry ass and make him pay." Vince vented his anger as he inched across the yard. Earl situated him into the other side of the backseat, wiring his handcuffed wrists to the other outside handle.

Jerry opened the passenger door on Ted's car and held up the vials of morphine he found on the seat. "Pretty clever."

Earl pulled out a swath of duct tape and, using his teeth, tore off a section.

"I've heard about enough out of both of you." He planted it across Vince's mouth then went around to the other side of the car and did the same to Bobby.

Moving away from the car, Earl addressed himself to Vera. "You know, there's no chance that Johnny's truck will resurface. Not filled with a ton of rifles."

He studied her face and continued, "I'll contact a friend of mine in Pierre who does some diving. See if he can recover Johnny's body."

"Thanks, Earl. I appreciate that." Vera nodded. "Guess I need to contact his next of kin? Not sure who that'd be?"

"If you're OK, Vera?" Earl looked concerned, then with a grin, added. "We're going to take this circus to town."

Earl winked at her as he got into the car. "You'll stop by sometime and tell Thelma the whole story? Nothing she likes better than a good story."

Vera watched as Earl headed off the property. The passengers in the backseat were bumped along with their arms extended out the window, wrists tied to the outside door handles. Jerry followed in Ted's car, leaving the Lincoln for Vera to drive back to Fort Thompson. Her Bug was parked at the tribal office.

She opened the front door of the big car. It was hot, dusty and smelled of cigarettes -- and stinky feet. She looked over the seat into the back. There on the floor of the backseat were two pairs of shoes.

## Chapter 43

Vera climbed out of the Lincoln and walked up the steps in front of the tribal office. Through the window she saw unfamiliar men, two in tribal uniforms and two in plain-clothes.

James looked up when she came in and met her at the door. "Geez, Vera, your face. Ya OK?"

"Oh yeah." She reached up to touch her still tender cheek. "Got a couple of stitches too." With all that had happened, she had forgotten about her injuries.

"How's Howard?"

"He'll be OK. Thank goodness the wound was superficial. Grazed his shoulder." The conversations in the office pushed them close together.

James leaned in and asked, "You found Johnny's partners?"

"We did. Earl and Jerry are taking them up to Miller." Vera surveyed the activity in the room. "How's it going here? Looks like the help you needed earlier has now arrived?"

James looked over his shoulder. "They intercepted Randall and the AIM leaders. They'll be talking with everyone involved in the trafficking of guns on the reservation."

Vera could see William sitting in a corner, his head hanging. Janet sat next to him. It looked like they were waiting for William's turn to talk with the authorities.

James turned back to her. "Any chance you'd give me a ride out to pick up my truck? It's down at the cabin by the river."

She walked beside James as he moved slowly down the front steps.

"We should get you checked out at the clinic, James?" She looked up at him with her eyebrows furrowed.

"I've got bruised ribs. Nothing to do about it." He carefully got into the passenger seat.

It was hot in the Bug. She reached over and rolled down the windows in the back.

"I never took this AIM business seriously." James was looking out the window. He continued, "I should've known, what with all the rumors going around."

Vera glanced at his worried face. "I still can't believe that Johnny set up a deal to sell AIM weapons."

It was quiet between them for a few minutes.

James looked over at her suddenly, with a half smile. "I called my folks when I got back to the office. Talked to my dad. He said he guessed they must of just missed Martha stopping by."

He chuckled a little. "Said they'd decided to take a little camping trip. Kinda last minute. Up on a remote part of Lower Brule."

"Ha. The grapevine comes through again."

She took her eyes off the road to look at him and ask. "Martha seems pretty determined?"

"She's all talk." James shook his head, a disgusted look on his face. "I doubt she'll be back anytime soon."

When they got to the point on the bridge where Johnny had driven off, Vera stopped her Bug and stared out her window down at the dark water. "I guess, in the end, Johnny wanted to redeem himself."

They continued on to the cabin, that was once again deserted. They got out of the car and walked to the river's edge. It was cooler next to the water. Small insects whirred in the reeds.

James broke the silence. "I haven't asked you yet for the details of yesterday."

She turned toward him, looked up and raised an eyebrow. "I could tell you about it later tonight?"

"That works for me." He looked down at her, smiled and pulled her into a hug.

"You smell good." She murmured, hugging back.

## Chapter 44

Vera had driven back to the ranch, done chores that needed doing, and had showered. She still had some time before the drive back to Fort Thompson.

She brought out the big box of pictures her mom kept in the back of a closet. Like at an archaeological site the pictures were layered chronologically, the earliest ones on the bottom. She dumped the contents of the box onto the dining room table and began to dig through them. After several minutes she found her parents as young adults. She sorted through that layer more slowly and found what she was looking for.


Vera got to James' house ahead of him. Waiting on the front step, absorbed with her thoughts, she didn't hear James drive up and park.

"Vera, you OK? Look like you've seen a ghost?"

She looked up, blinked, and handed him a photo. "I found this picture of Mom, Dad and Johnny."

He took a look at it. "They look so young."

James brought it up close for a longer look, then looked at her.

She took the photo back from him and stared at it.

Standing with her tall, blond, blue-eyed Dad, and her tall, dark haired, brown-eyed Mom, was a young man, short with a wiry build. Johnny's dark red hair was wild and curly, his face was covered with freckles, and he had a gappy-toothed smile.

She looked up, confused. "I guess I don't know who Johnny was?"

Vera stood at the sink peeling potatoes. She'd needed a distraction.

James stood next to her, cleaning and chopping vegetables for a salad. He glanced at her. "I'm happy to see you working in my kitchen."

She looked up at him, startled out of her reverie, and smiled. "It's nice to be here."

He dried his hands. "Let's have a look at your head."

She felt his breath on her scalp as he gently parted her hair. "Ya know I could probably take out those stitches in a few days, if you want?"

She turned around to face him. "Seems you are talented in many respects."

"Glad ya noticed." He smiled down at her.

She continued, "And it seems to me we make a pretty good crime-fighting team."

"I agree." His eyes crinkled with his smile. "Are you changing your mind about life in a small town?"

"Maybe I am?" she held his gaze and thought a minute. "Life in a small town is small."

She added with a smile of her own. "It's also surprising."

After a long kiss, which felt both familiar and inviting, Vera drew back to look up at James. "And it's something I might be able to get used to."

## Elsa's Rhubarb Bread

1 ½ Cup brown sugar
1 ½  Cup oil
1 egg
1 tsp vanilla
1 tsp soda
½  tsp baking powder
1 tsp salt
2 ½ Cups flour
1 Cup buttermilk (substitute milk with 1 tsp of vinegar in it)
1 ½ Cups rhubarb (diced)
½ Cup chopped walnuts
½ Cup white sugar
2 Tbsp butter

Cream sugar and oil, then add egg and vanilla.

Mix dry ingredients together, add to mixture alternating with the buttermilk.

Add rhubarb and nuts.

Put in 2 greased and floured bread pans.

Sprinkle ½ Cup sugar on top (¼ on each)

Pour 2 Tbsp melted butter on sugar (1 Tbsp on each).

Bake at 325 degrees for 60 minutes or more. Do not underbake.

1.

33657524R00173

Made in the USA
Lexington, KY
13 March 2019